Tillmon County Fire

Tillmon County Fire

Pamela Ehrenberg

Eerdmans Books for Young Readers

Grand Rapids, Michigan / Cambridge, U.K.

Text © 2009 Pamela Ehrenberg

Published in 2009 by Eerdmans Books for Young Readers,
an imprint of Wm. B. Eerdmans Publishing Co.

Wm. B. Eerdmans Publishing Co. '
2140 Oak Industrial Dr. NE, Grand Rapids, Michigan 49505
P.O. Box 163, Cambridge CB3 9PU U.K.

www.eerdmans.com/youngreaders

Manufactured in the United States of America

13 12 11 10 09   7 6 5 4 3 2 1

Library of Congress Cataloging-in-Publication Data

Ehrenberg, Pamela.
  Tillmon County fire / by Pamela Ehrenberg.
    p.   cm.
      Summary: An act of arson committed as an anti-gay hate crime
    affects the lives of several teenagers from a small town.
      ISBN 978-0-8028-5345-5 (pbk: alk. paper)
  [1. Arson — Fiction. 2. Hate crimes — Fiction. 3. Community life —
  Small town — Fiction.]
    I. Title.

  PZ7.E3233Ti 2009
  [Fic] — dc22
                                    2008022102

In Eric's memory,
and in honor of our children,
Talia Sage and Nathan Eric

Contents

Prologue

Cait

Getting to Tillmon County is easy: go west on the interstate until you think you'll fall off the edge of the earth,
then turn left. What's hard is that after about five minutes, any person of reasonable intelligence will start to
wonder what's the point.

The tourism bureau says the mountain scenery is the
point, and it's true that there's about a week in mid-
October when the trees burst out with so many red and
orange and yellow leaves that a person could be forgiven for enjoying the show and not believing that it's
really all about death. But then November comes and
Route 329 ices over, and you're left wondering all over
again.

Older people say their family is the point. Their relatives have lived in Tillmon County since Joseph Stenton moved out here in 1855, following what can only be described as a scandal involving his relationship with Henry Tillmon, the future state senator. (This fact is generally not talked about except by people like me who live too far out in the sticks for high-speed Internet and therefore go poking around in the Historical Society for social studies projects instead of copying something from Wikipedia like everyone else. You can tell who won and who lost in that little relationship drama, because Stenton Road, leading into the metropolis of Spruce Valley, has only two lanes, and the most exciting things about it are the Agway and Krafts by Kimberlyn — but before he died Joseph Stenton managed to get the whole damn county named after his friend. Personally, I'd have been more than a little annoyed if I had to move way out here while my friend continued on his rise to state government as if I'd never existed, but maybe I'll see it differently if I'm ever in love.)

■ ■ ■

Recently, though, I've been preoccupied with bigger things than love: some things about my family and some things about a fire last spring at one of those enormous houses near Lake Albright. I'm holding a clipping about that in my hand right now, a page from the *Tillmon Register* where the article about Aiden McNalley and the arson is surrounded by stories about milk prices and the middle school spelling champions.

I can look at this page, this news about the trial and all the background noise around it, and I can say that this is my life, and also the life of a lot of other young and old and church-going and non-church-going and hard-working and not-so-hard-working people who live in Tillmon County and places just like it. It's my life, but it's their life too. We're in this together, however we might feel about each other at any particular moment. And remembering that makes me think, at least for a little while, that maybe I've found the point.

Getting Saved

Aiden

For four weeks I worked as a counselor at the Church of the Holy Redeemer's Vacation Bible School, because they had a van that would pick me up in Mount Jenkins when they picked up campers by the lake, and there aren't many summer jobs that don't require you to have your own transportation. Being that I didn't care much about (1) kids, or (2) the Holy Redeemer, *I* wouldn't have hired me for the counselor job, but looking back, I can see that Pastor Paul had an eye out for people who needed the Lord.

I helped the kids on and off the van, which was driven by Pastor Paul's wife, Debbie, and I told the kids to sit down and not throw stuff from their lunch boxes. Most of their parents were taking a vacation on the lake and had signed them up without thinking too much about the Holy Redeemer or anything other than someone else watching their kids while they jet-skied around the lake and got drunk on good liquor. So even rich parents wanted to get rid of their kids; that was enlightening to know.

The second week, the last kid dropped off in the afternoon was a little guy named Toby, maybe four or six years old. Every day he fell asleep on the van ride back to the big vacation house, then he'd wake up and stumble inside. He looked like my dad tripping in the door, trying to figure out how the hell he ended up there.

But on Toby's last day, he stayed asleep when the van stopped.

So I got up and said, "Hey, Toby," and when he kept sleeping, I put my hand on his shoulder. And he woke up and looked hung over and stumbled off the van like usual.

Except I left one part out. When my hand was on his shoulder, I thought about something I hadn't thought of for a very long time. I thought about how from the end of first grade until the beginning of third, when my mother died, I rode home with her from this after-school day care near her job, and I remember almost nothing about it except the long ride, how I would always be asleep when we got home and my mother would wake me up with a kiss on the cheek.

But it was my fault, not my mother's, that I leaned over and brushed my lips over Toby's cheek.

I looked up real quick, but Debbie was messing with the radio dial and hadn't seen anything. And then Toby was out of the van, down the driveway, about to get swallowed up by that fourteen-karat designer-grade monster of a house.

I couldn't sleep all weekend, which was too bad, because when my dad runs out of money at the end of the month, he hangs around the house looking to start fights, and sleeping is usually one of my best escapes. Sunday night I almost got hit by one of my mother's ceramic birds that he threw across the room.

On Monday, Pastor Paul asked about my relationship with Jesus Christ. At first I thought the timing was just a coincidence, but now I know better. The truth was that Jesus Christ and I had not had much of a relationship recently. My mother had brought me to church when I was a kid, and I didn't see much point in going without her. Also, since Jesus Christ had my mother for company where they were, I had no reason to take up His time down here.

But Pastor Paul started me seeing things differently, like I could keep in touch better with my dead mother by getting to know her friend Jesus. Pastor Paul and I talked the rest of the summer during arts and crafts, while the kids made crosses out of Popsicle sticks and yarn. Pastor Paul talked about Jesus like He was someone who worked at the Agway, someone who'd load your truck up for you without you having to ask.

At first, I didn't pray over it exactly; I just closed my eyes and tried talking to my mom, telling her I was sorry for how things turned out. She didn't talk back, not like voices in my head or anything, but I started to get the idea that my dad's drinking and the way we lived — that maybe some of that wasn't my fault. It was a funny kind of peacefulness, kind of like I remembered from my mom picking me up at day care and asking about my day, before I fell asleep in the car.

But just like alcohol and nicotine, peacefulness can get addictive. Soon five minutes in chapel isn't enough, and you start craving peaceful moments before bed, or waiting for the van in the morning, or hiding out from a crazy dad. You start wishing you could feel peaceful like that all the time, and you're willing to do almost anything to get there. So when someone tells you there's a way to always be that peaceful, plus after you die you're guaranteed to see your mom again, no matter what kind of stupid stuff you did — all that sounds pretty good, especially over the noise of your dad smashing bottles on the back porch.

So in August, I got saved. I just stood up one Sunday during the service, at the quiet part when everyone closed their eyes and Pastor Paul asked who was ready. Suddenly I wasn't just a screwed-up troublemaker nobody wanted around. Suddenly I had a purpose.

Each week, on the last day of camp, we wrote down our sins on these green strips of paper. Then Pastor Paul and Bill Sherman, who worked at the camp as a groundskeeper and handyman, built a bonfire and we tossed our sins into the flames. Each week, the flames were stronger and more powerful, like they were remembering and transforming our messes into something holy. If I stared long enough, I could almost imagine that the fire held a sliver of heaven's eternal light.

■ ■ ■

But I should have known that like everything else, this peacefulness was temporary. After camp ended, I started to wonder about Pastor Paul's bit about loving all of God's children and the value of all human beings. If we were all so good and worthy, how could we have sinned enough to fuel all those fires? That didn't sit right with me.

So I went online and found some people who told it more like it was, who faced the parts of the Bible that would never make it into a craft project with yarn and Popsicle sticks. Finally I started to understand what I saw all around me, not just from living with my father, but from living where rich tourists come to jet-ski half a mile from where perfectly good people work their butts off their whole lives and still can't get their kids enough to eat. It wasn't bad luck that made the world this way; it was Evil. Which maybe was worse, I don't know. But unlike luck, Evil could be taken on. I saw now that I wouldn't have to search far to find Evil, just turn on the radio or walk past the dirty magazines at the Quik-Mart or Little Joe's. Evil was everywhere; I just had to be alert to its disguises.

It snowed right before Thanksgiving, and the Church of the Holy Redeemer looked like a freaking postcard, all clean and pure. But it got me nervous, thinking about what was underneath. I kept imagining my sins and the sins of everyone else in this county moldering and rotting all winter without ever drying out enough to burn. It would take a blowtorch to sear through the snow and reveal what was underneath. Every flake of snow made me want to punch a hole through one of those little church windows, like my own blood could bring the world closer to those peaceful flames.

The roads iced over and people in Tillmon County huddled inside, knowing that their lives were uninterrupted until the first thaw. And as long as the snow was on the ground, the thought of going back to that little postcard church with the stupid icicles in the windows made my heart pound and my palms sweat. I just couldn't do it, no matter how many times Pastor Paul invited me or how much free pizza they served at the Sunday night teen fellowship meetings. And the longer I stayed away, the more I read in the Bible and on the Internet, and I realized what was wrong with Pastor Paul. He was so big on loving everyone, he'd have us love the Devil himself if he came to town. Because whether Pastor Paul knew it or not, Tillmon County was not too small for the Devil to bother with. And it didn't matter how strong or weak I felt, or whether I had a church behind me: I had to fight back.

At first I didn't know how I'd do it. But in January,

when Rob Sullivan moved into one of the mansions on the same street where Toby had stayed, and started prancing and lisping around Tillmon County High School, I knew. That month, we had thirty-three inches of snow. But I wasn't afraid anymore, because I understood that after the snow, spring would come. When the snow melted, I would be ready.

Yellowbelly Falls

Ben

The first time I found the synagogue, I was driving back from Home Depot with plywood and paint for a new birdhouse. There was a detour on the interstate, so I had to go through downtown Carter Springs, and at the corner of Grant and Washington I saw the old stone building with six-pointed stars on the windows. The stars reminded me of my father's prayer book, the one from before he decided God didn't live in this part of the country and wandered off to look for Him. So I pulled into the parking lot.

It was eleven-thirty on a Saturday morning, in the middle of a service, and I slipped into a seat in the back. The prayer book, unlike my father's, was half in English, and the songs were mostly about how great God is: catching the falling, freeing the fettered, that sort of thing. The old lady sitting a few feet away from me seemed to be writing in her prayer book, taking notes or something, but when I stood up, I saw she was working on a crossword puzzle torn out from the *Carter Springs Ledger*. I liked the synagogue better after that.

■ ■ ■

From about a mile out of Spruce Valley, past Food Fair and Owenbraun's Chevrolet, Tillmon County is just mountains the whole forty-eight miles to the interstate. Sometimes you can hear National Public Radio from Pittsburgh, but not many people know about that, or care. Maybe a girl could get away with listening, but a seventeen-year-old guy who liked NPR had to listen when no one was around. If I timed things right on a Saturday, I could listen to "This American Life" on the drive up to Carter Springs and "Car Talk" coming home. My cat, Spike, didn't like me being gone all day on a weekend, so she'd usually sulk for an hour when I got home before letting me rub her head and back to make up for it.

When I was a kid, my family sometimes went to the movies in Carter Springs, one county over. We'd leave around ten in the morning, and my parents would see one movie and my sisters would fight over who had to sit with me in the kids' movie and who could smoke in the parking lot with their friends. We'd stop at Wendy's on the way up and Dairy Queen on the way back, neither of which we have in Tillmon County, and we'd get home around five in the afternoon. My sisters played Ben-pong in the back seat, taking turns pushing me back and forth, and I'd look out the sliver of front window between my parents' seats, feeling nauseous from the greasy food and giddy at the same time.

We kept up the drives for awhile after my sisters moved out of the house, one studying to be a physical therapy assistant and one living near Morgantown with two babies. But greasy fast food was one of the first things to go when my father found God, the year I was twelve. He stopped eating animals that didn't chew their cud and have split hooves, like

9

it said in the Bible. Then the Saturday drives ended, because my father could do no manner of work on the Jewish Sabbath, even turning over the ignition in the car.

My father being half-Jewish had been no big deal until his mother, my Grandma Lois, died. My dad left the house for hours, sometimes all day. One morning I found him in the living room, holding a prayer book and rocking back and forth. I got some cookies from the kitchen and snuck back upstairs, and later I found his prayer book behind some old photo albums. I hoped it might tell me what was wrong with him, but it was all in some crazy language that didn't even use normal letters. Hebrew, I figured, like the ancient people in the desert spoke. I squinted at the funny marks on the page, in case they had some all-but-lost secrets for talking to God. After my father left, I looked for the prayer book again, but of course he had taken it with him.

Plenty of people do things for their religion, I guess, so for a while we just thought my father was exploring a side of himself we hadn't seen before. But six months into his transformation, he had grown a beard and started dressing only in black and white, almost Amish-looking except for the little cap called a yarmulke on his head. By then, we almost couldn't recognize my father on the outside, and it was getting harder to recognize him on the inside. He wouldn't eat off our dishes, and once, when my Aunt Phyllis (a woman to whom he was not related by blood) kissed him on the cheek to say "happy birthday," he recoiled like she had stabbed him with the cake knife. Sometime around then, even my sixth-grade self knew this was not ordinary, God-fearing behavior. He left us three months later, listening to some imagined booming voice of God.

···

All this about birdhouses and NPR and my father finding God sounds pretty screwed up, even to me, so I should probably mention I have a girlfriend. Her name is Amelia, and even though she thinks she's all different from the people around here, dating her is about the most normal thing I've ever done.

She thinks she's so different because she was born in China and adopted when she was a baby. It's true Tillmon County doesn't have a lot of Asians, maybe just Amelia and the pharmacist's wife and the new dentist at the Health Clinic, and you have to drive past Carter Springs to Flanders if you want sushi — but sushi isn't Chinese, it's Japanese, and Amelia won't even eat the kind with raw fish, she'll just nibble on a cucumber roll and then want to stop at Friendly's for a brownie sundae. Which is not the point, but she doesn't speak Chinese, and she eats what everybody else eats and dresses like all the other girls (tight sweaters in the winter, skimpy halter tops in the summer, stuff that's supposed to look sexy, I guess). The point is, she's not as different as she thinks.

When she first asked me out, right before Halloween, I knew it was a terrible idea, but I also thought maybe if I went out with Amelia, all kinds of things about me would magically change. I could transform myself into the kind of person who goes out with Amelia, the kind of person whose father comes home to a happy, normal family. And now that we're dating, it would take too much effort to stop. We've seen movies in Carter Springs and gone out for pizza; we've also held hands at assemblies and kissed in the hallway, but that's about it, if you get what I'm saying. I mean, yeah, I'm curious what it's like, and sometimes we'll be kissing and I'll think, I wouldn't mind finding out right *now* what it's like. But mostly I'm not in a big hurry, which is maybe the biggest proof that I will never be normal.

■ ■ ■

There's a new guy, Rob, at school this year, which should have been a red flag to begin with, because who moves to Tillmon County in the middle of junior year? But Rob showed up with rumors that he moved here from New York to live with his aunt while his parents joined the Peace Corps, or that his dad was an oil tycoon in Brazil or something crazy like that.

Usually I'm not so into rumors. I figure the more involved I get with other people, the more questions they'll ask about me, like why am I spending so much time around Jews and when am I going to screw my girlfriend, stuff like that. There are a few people I'll nod hi to in the halls, but I don't have a lot of what you'd call friends. But with Rob I got curious, maybe because he was the first proof I had that New York City really existed. And then he showed up in my physics class, and I knew we'd become friends whether we wanted to or not.

This was what he looked like that first day: brown curly hair, longer than curly-haired guys usually wear their hair. Two earrings, barely visible behind the curls: a gold hoop on one side and a diamond stud in the other. Gray eyes, light enough that I could tell what color they were even from across the aisle. Plaid shirt in a soft-looking cotton, not from Wal-Mart and definitely not from Ogleby's Outdoor Shop ("whatever your sport, whatever your game, come down to Ogleby's at Third and Main"). A nice, easy smile, and a little dimple like a reward.

A week later, when my lab partner got sick with mono, Rob was assigned to work with me.

"Hi," he said. I had thought New Yorkers talked all hurried, but Rob talked nice and slow. And not like Tillmon County men who talk slow because they have nothing better to do than stand outside Agway and talk about milk prices, but more like he was confident you'd want to stick around and listen. And he was right: I would have stuck around even to hear him talk about milk.

In a lab situation, the harder you concentrate on making sure your hand doesn't accidentally brush someone else's, the less it matters if your hands actually touch or not, because you can feel a weird sort of buzzing when your hands are three or four inches apart. I could have avoided it, could have made sure my hands were nowhere near his, but I didn't. He didn't either. Did prisoners feel that kind of buzzing right before they sat in the electric chair?

■ ■ ■

One Friday in February, our lab assignment was to fill a two-liter pop bottle with water and flip it back and forth to see which way an air bubble accelerates. It didn't necessarily mean anything when Rob bonked me on the elbow with our

13

bottle; he was just being goofy, and I bonked him back, letting the plastic bottle linger on the back of his hand. Then he flicked my sleeve, and chills raced through my body.

He said, smiling, "You got Wite-Out or something on your shirt."

Thank God for the noise of twenty-four other kids and their pop bottles, so nobody other than Rob saw my face turn bright red. I had been waiting for this moment and dreading it my whole life.

"What?" he said. "There's worse things than Wite-Out." Rob's dimple twitched, inviting me into something, like quicksand.

I glanced at my sleeve, even though I already knew what was there.

"Actually, it's bird crap," I said. If anyone, anywhere has ever said anything dumber, it's hard to imagine.

Rob laughed. "Like that Far Side cartoon where the bird sees everybody as target practice?"

"Sort of. Although birds actually have better vision than humans." That fast, I beat my own record for the dumbest comment ever made.

"Really?" said Rob. "Even pigeons?"

"I don't know much about pigeons." I picked up the bottle and tilted it back and forth, watching the air bubble slide back and forth.

"That's pretty much the only bird you see in New York."

"Huh."

"Where do you go to watch birds?" Rob asked. Across the room, someone dropped a pop bottle and it bounced a couple of times on the floor.

14

"Well — " my voice caught a little. "Well, this time of year, there aren't many. But the best chance is around Yellowbelly Falls."

"Huh," Rob said, looking at me. I held that pop bottle so tightly I thought the plastic might crack.

Then I heard my voice saying, "We could . . . if you want, I could show you. If you want to know where the birds are."

"I do," said Rob.

I wanted this more than I had ever wanted anything. Also less than I had ever wanted anything. If I started down this path, I might never find my way off. The room was suddenly freezing.

I said, "Maybe, I don't know, Sunday? Around noon?"

Rob smiled, taunting me with that dimple. "You don't think that's too public?"

City people are like that, thinking anything not in a sealed-up building is public. When the falls are practically the only place in the county loud enough to hide a conversation.

I said, "No, it's Midcreek Falls that gets all the tourists. And that's only in the summer."

I glanced around, but nobody was paying attention.

"Well, I'm not the one who minds public," Rob said.

■ ■ ■

Most Saturdays, I would think up errands that could only be done in Carter Springs, like stocking up on giant bags of kitty litter. Then I'd drive up there and go to the synagogue. Synagogue: even the word felt solid, like the stone building and the polished wooden benches anchored to the floor. The foreign chanting made me think I could ask God some questions, get his opinion on things. Talking to God was like talking to Spike in that you couldn't expect much of an answer. Also, they both liked being buttered up first, either by telling them how great they are (God) or rubbing their head (Spike).

Um, God? Even if you don't know everything, you probably know some things, right? So could you fill me in a little about why I'm this way? Or if you can't tell me that, can you at least confirm you did it on purpose?

God? It's okay that you didn't answer before. But those bumper stickers about how you made Adam and Eve, not Adam and Steve — I mean, does anyone know for sure? Or are they just guessing?

God? I get that you're not going to answer. But it's not because I'm in Tillmon County, right? I mean, the thing about my dad leaving the state to find you — aren't you supposed to be everywhere?

■ ■ ■

The first Sunday hike was cold and damp, with patches of snow all through the woods. We saw white-throated sparrows and shared granola mix I had packed and Oreo cookies Rob brought. He told me about New York, about having to move for his dad's job. He thought the oil-tycoon-in-Brazil rumor was funny. I told Rob about the synagogue in Carter Springs and my dad being half-Jewish, but I didn't mention him leaving to find God.

At the falls, we sat on a flat, wet rock. It had started to

16

drizzle, and we were at least two hours from the park entrance.

Looking at the falls, Rob asked, "What do the Jews of Carter Springs think about gay people?"

I looked at the water. It felt like the rock we were sitting on might hurtle into the falls and off the face of the earth.

"I don't know. They're Reform Jews, so I think they're pretty modern."

I looked at him sideways. A few drops of rain had settled on his curly hair, each drop its own little universe.

"How about you?" he asked. The falls and the rain were so loud, his voice sounded like a whisper. "Are you pretty modern?"

When I didn't answer, he took my hand. His fingers were warm.

I could have stayed there forever, but our socks were getting wet, so when Rob scooted to the edge of the rock and looked at me like did I want to head back, I nodded and followed him to the trail. We held hands like that the whole way, just our fingers curled around each other, except for a couple of slippery places where we had to steady ourselves with branches.

"Thanks for showing me this place," he said at the end. He ran his fingers through his hair to dry it.

"Yeah," I said. "There's lots more trails, so when it's not raining . . ."

"Maybe next Sunday," he said. "If you don't have plans."

■ ■ ■

So that was how we started hiking around Yellowbelly Falls every Sunday. As spring arrived, we saw more warblers, lots of sparrows, of course, and once, an American goldfinch. We hiked even when it rained, which was a lot that spring. I told my mom I had joined a hiking group from school.

"It's sort of a new group," I said.

"That's wonderful," she said. I heard her tell my Aunt Phyllis on the phone that I had finally joined a club, that Aunt Phyllis had been right about late bloomers. Spike looked at me like a conspirator.

By April it was still chilly but not completely crazy to be out in the woods without a jacket, or without a shirt. We found hidden spaces between the trees. It wasn't my plan, but lying on a towel surrounded by cool, moist air, the sound of the falls, and the downy hair on Rob's chest was pretty much a perfect way to experience nature.

For the first time since my dad left, I didn't feel like a piece of me was missing. Neither father I knew — the mountain man's man I grew up with or the father who came along later, the one who cared more about his God than his family — neither of them would have stomached me and Rob alone together, at the falls or anywhere else. But for the first time in my life, something was more right than my father.

It wasn't my plan, but when the time came, I didn't feel any of the same hesitation I had with Amelia. It was right, even if it wasn't, and when it was over, I finally understood what people had been going crazy after all these years. It wasn't his first time, I could tell, both from the way he held me and because I'm pretty sure you can't buy a Day-Glo condom within a hundred miles of Tillmon County. But I remembered a country music song I heard sometimes on the radio: *"I don't care if I'm your first love, as long as I'm your last."* Nobody else had ever made me want to quote country music.

■ ■ ■

When I was eight, I hung pinecones outside and spread them with different kinds of peanut butter to see what the birds liked best. After that I started building simple birdhouses from kits you could get at Miller's Hardware. My dad tried to help, but he got frustrated when I cared more about what kind of peanut butter the birds liked than about using the electric drill. That was probably the first clue that I was different from how boys are supposed to be.

I hung the birdhouses every year until I was twelve, when my father went looking for God. Then one morning that February a blackpoll warbler showed up on my windowsill, like it remembered the peanut butter from the year before. It hopped around while I got ready for school, and Spike sat on my bed, calculating. I smiled for the first time in months.

But when I rode my bike to the Quik-Mart to buy more peanut butter, the lottery jackpot was at a record high and I had to wait in line a long time behind people buying tickets. Which is when I noticed, on the cover of a magazine called *Men's Health*, a man whose most distinguishing feature was not his good health but his skin-tight red bikini-bottom bathing suit. I turned away suddenly, not knowing how long I had looked at the magazine but sure that everyone in the store had seen me looking at it. But then I didn't know where else to look. My eyes darted around, and I felt my face get hotter as I shifted the jar of peanut butter in front of me. There, standing in line at the Quik-Mart, which had maybe ten or twelve magazines with girls in bikinis that I had never paid any attention to, I finally understood what it was that made me different.

My hands shook while I paid for the peanut butter, and twice on the bike ride home I almost wiped out by the side of the road but regained my balance just in time. Since then, I have fed the birds every winter but avoided shopping at the Quik-Mart.

■ ■ ■

After the hikes started, I still saw Amelia on Saturday nights, but that was pretty much it. She thought my Saturday mornings were for helping my mom with errands, and Sunday afternoons were for homework and birdhouses. I felt so guilty about lying that I bought her a completely inappropriate red heart brooch that the store must have had left over from Valentine's Day. I could tell she hated it, and I hated myself for giving it to her. Maybe I was trying to drum up enough feelings for her so we could finally break up.

Which I might have done if Rob hadn't caught up with me in the parking lot one Friday after school.

"Hey," he said.

I couldn't help it, I looked around to see who was watching.

"*This* they can't have us arrested for," Rob said. "Even here."

I smiled a little, but I still felt like everyone knew, like seeing us talking in the parking lot was the same as seeing us at the falls.

"I wanted to tell you that my great-uncle's sick."

Of course, I assumed he was canceling our hike that weekend. Which was one step removed from canceling me, canceling this whole thing. That was probably how he was, probably how everyone was in New York: stick around for the conquest, then move on. For just a second, I imagined my life without Rob, without looking over my shoulder every minute.

"Sorry to hear that," I said in what I hoped was a stoic voice.

"Yeah, I never met him. But my parents are away this weekend. So if your mom would believe the school hiking club has an overnight hike . . ."

I steadied myself against the bumper of someone's truck. Was Rob asking me to sleep over?

He laughed and said, "The falls at noon?"

And even though later I replayed the scene in my head with a thousand different endings, the real ending was that I nodded.

■ ■ ■

Over lasagna that night, I told my mom about the overnight hike. I waited for her to question my story, but her face glowed with the imagined scenario of me finally fitting in, with her being able to laugh and joke about Tillmon sports with the other mothers at Food Fair.

So she said of course I could go, and I said I thought I had mentioned the trip before. She was all flustered and smiling: not only was I doing normal teenage things, but I was forgetting to tell my mom about them. She couldn't have been prouder.

But I wanted to dig a hole under my bed and disappear. I couldn't sleep. I stared at the ceiling, but instead of quiet in my head I kept hearing the stupid pop songs they played over and over on KXZ until you wanted to punch a hole through your speakers. I pulled the pillow tight around my ears, and finally, to drive out the music, I started playing the synagogue service in my mind. I was surprised at how much I remembered, even though I didn't know Hebrew and I never sang along. Did Jews even believe in Hell? Either way, I couldn't imagine my father being happy, if he came back from wherever he was and found me like this.

Hey, God? Is this your sick idea of a joke?

If it wasn't for Rob, life could be as simple as the birdhouse kits from Miller's Hardware, as simple as having my deepest, darkest secret be that I was part Jewish. I could get a scholarship to Flanders State, where nobody cared what I was: Jewish, semi-Jewish, a bird-watching physics major who thinks about other guys. In Flanders I bet nobody wore T-shirts that said "love the sinner, hate the sin," and third-graders didn't play games called "smear the queer."

Rob thought he was so great because he was from New York, but what did he know? New York didn't even have birds other than pigeons. It was one thing holding each other in the woods, where an hour later we could pretend nothing ever happened. But going to his house, spending the night — that was different. If I spent the night, this thing would stop being

a half-dream that happened by the falls and would start being something real. That was scarier than anything. (Anything? Scarier than the idea of my father never coming back?
Well, as scary, anyway.)

But if I didn't spend the night — if I stopped things right
now — maybe this could still be something I played around
with as a kid, something I'd tell my wife about one day.
(Amelia? No, not Amelia. If I had to imagine a wife, I imagined a nameless, faceless nobody.)

Until I met Rob, I hadn't even understood how a body and
brain could have such opposite demands. My body's insis-
tence terrified me. How could I spend the night at Rob's
house? But how could I not? And who did he think he was, asking this of me?

Before I went to sleep, I prayed to the Jewish God for rain
and the cancellation of the imaginary hiking club overnight.
But my body, or more specifically my left hand, invalidated
my prayers.

■ ■ ■

Or maybe God decided I wasn't really Jewish, because Saturday morning was foggy but not the kind of weather you'd
cancel a hike over. For my mom, I had to make a big show of
leaving the house, carrying a sleeping bag to the car and listening to her go on about brushing my teeth. Probably she'd
been waiting years to bug me about that.

I drove to Carter Springs with the radio off, just rolled the
window down and listened to the road. The faster I drove,
the more the road noise sounded like waterfalls, so it was a

relief to pull off the exit and park in the synagogue parking lot. Until I realized, like an idiot, that I was dressed for an imaginary hiking trip, wearing my oldest jeans and a ratty sweatshirt. Not even a Gentile could go in like that, so I sat in the car with the window down. The windows with the six-pointed stars were open, tilted up, and I could hear parts of the service escaping into the parking lot.

Would my father be glad I was in a synagogue parking lot? And that I sometimes went in and talked to God? Or would he be so disgusted by what I talked to God about that the kind of parking lot wouldn't matter?

After synagogue, I stopped at Lowe's Garden Center and bought a dozen Gerbera daisies, Amelia's favorite. Then I turned the car back toward Tillmon County.

■ ■ ■

"You remembered!" Amelia squealed when she saw the flowers, like her perfectly normal boyfriend was bringing her perfectly normal flowers. She didn't comment on how I was dressed.

"Yeah, well, it was nice out. I felt like riding to Carter Springs — "

"You drove to Carter Springs to get me flowers? That is so sweet! I was wondering where you found these, because Newman's never has anything. Like, this one time, I was looking for, well, whatever. Let me put these in water! Do you want a drink? Lemonade or Pepsi?"

I drank Pepsi while Amelia told me her parents had driven to Pittsburgh to go to an art museum. I tried to remember where Rob's great-uncle lived, if the two sets of parents were at that moment cruising the same highway.

"They wanted me to come, but I was like, hello, I have homework, it's not like I can be this perfect student or whatever if you never give me time to study. And art museums? Blah! So they let me stay home, and then of course I totally couldn't concentrate. So, it's perfect that you're here."

Rob would have given up on me coming on our hike. He would have waited near the entrance to the falls, wondering whether I'd wrecked my car, and eventually gone home. Or maybe he hiked by himself, walking past all our spots, stopping at the rock where we had sat and talked that first day. He wasn't crazy enough to jump off that rock into the falls; people only die for each other if they're in love, and we hadn't said anything about love.

Amelia was saying, "I don't think you've ever been here before when my parents weren't home."

"Really?" She knew I knew that.

"Yeah," she said. "Do you want — I don't know — do you want a tour?" She flipped her hair in a way that told me what kind of tour she had in mind.

I imagined Rob by himself at the falls, and my father by himself somewhere, looking for God. Me by myself building birdhouses, talking to Spike, driving to Carter Springs. Amelia by herself, waiting for me to finish hiking with Rob.

We stood up, and I tossed my Pepsi can into a blue-lined recycling bin.

I started, "I'm — "

She looked at me. I'm what? What am I, anyway?

"I'm sorry for not being around much lately."

"You're here now," she said.

Amelia lived twelve miles from Yellowbelly Falls. If I drove about a million miles an hour, maybe I could catch up with Rob as he was leaving.

"Yeah," I said. I put my hand on Amelia's waist and followed her up the stairs.

california

amelia

friday, april 21

surfbuddy isn't online. surfbuddy is always online. it's
1:37 a.m., which is only 10:37 in california. i IM him:

important! where r u?

on weather.com, i check malibu, beverly hills, and
coconut beach, which is near san diego and is where
surfbuddy lives. it's not famous, but surfbuddy says
it's very sunny and has plenty of asian people. i imagine everyone in california looking like me, even though
i know there are tons of mexicans and probably even
more blond-haired, blue-eyed people than i've ever
seen in my life. still, california has lots of asian people. i already know one: a half-korean, half-filipino boy
named surfbuddy.

hello???

california has people from china, where i was adopted from, and japanese people, which i might be part, plus koreans and filipinos, plus vietnamese, plus south asians, who don't look anything like me but who count anyway. when i was adopted at age six months, i doubled tillmon county's asian population, the pharmacist's wife being the one and only asian person here for like twenty years. since then five other asians have lived here, but not at the same time.

big news @ apt!!!

i click back on the coconut beach real estate site for another look at my perfect apartment. it's a one-bedroom basement apartment, on a hill, so it gets lots of light. surfbuddy has promised that if i find an apartment, he'll check it out for me and even lend me money for the deposit. i'll pay him back, of course, just like i'll pay my parents back for the plane ticket, which i'll have to buy using their credit card. if you pay it back, it's just borrowing, right? it's okay to borrow if you're desperate.

a window pops up on my screen:

surfbudd3: hey
melicious: i found an apt!!!
surfbudd3: for real?
melicious: 224 pacific ave! can u check it out?
surfbudd3: totally

melicious: hope we recognize each other when i
get there
surfbudd3: dont all of us look the same :)
melicious: lol
surfbudd3: i bet ur even prettier than those
pictures
melicious: shut up
surfbudd3: i can tell by how u type

four hours later, i'm attempting to get dressed for
school. if you are exactly five feet tall and weigh less
than a hundred pounds, there is seriously nowhere in
this county to buy clothes that fit, let alone clothes
to wear in an actual high school. and don't even get me
started on finding shoes in four-and-a-half narrow.
packing for california will be easy, because i'll have to
get all new clothes when i get there.

at school i spend all morning in honors classes i am
taking against my will. in fifth grade, i purposely
messed up the test to qualify for honors classes because i didn't want to spend seven years around kids
like paula delacorte, who wears the same clothes over
and over until they smell, and not because she's poor
either, but because she gets so distracted by science
fiction books that she forgets about planet earth.
    but i failed at failing the test.
    "i don't understand these results," my teacher
kept saying, while my parents squirmed in fifth-grade
desks. they're older parents, which is why they

adopted a baby from china to begin with, and they nodded at whatever she said, including how she would talk to the principal and try to get me in the honors classes anyway, on a trial basis.

that day, in the car on the way home, i screamed, "not all asian people are geniuses, you know!" and my mom said, "sweetie, this isn't about being asian, it's about making sure your schoolwork isn't too easy for you."

but nothing has ever been easy for me.

i met surfbuddy in a chat room on adoptedkids.com a few months ago.

february 15, 11:39 p.m.

> **surfbudd3:** do people where u live even know what china is?
> **melicious:** dont b retarded
> **surfbudd3:** sorry
> **surfbudd3:** how old r u?
> **melicious:** 17 u?
> **surfbudd3:** 17
> **surfbudd3:** not quite but soon
> **melicious:** how soon?
> **surfbudd3:** oct 9
> **surfbudd3:** next year
> **melicious:** funny
> **surfbudd3:** u should come 2 cali
> **melicious:** sure
> **melicious:** y not?

sometimes i hate that i have to leave. people act like tillmon county is some kind of hellhole, like living where you can leave your door unlocked and the motor running in downtown spruce valley while you stop in at third street bakery to buy a lemon tart on the way to school — like that's a fate worse than death or something. if it wasn't for this fear that you never knew when the next dumb comment might come, like someone saying how good my english is — even if comments like that only happen once every five years or so, it's enough to make me remember that sooner or later i have to leave, so i figure it might as well be sooner.

when abby peterschott turned nine, her birthday party had a california theme, which meant we ate pizza with ham and pineapple and did a disneyland scavenger hunt. when my dad picked me up at eight o'clock, i noticed that all the other kids getting picked up were boys, then i saw the pile of girls' sleeping bags inside the front door. my invitation had definitely said six to eight p.m., but maybe the invitation was a mistake, maybe i got one that was meant for a boy. i wanted to ask abby's mom, but my dad wouldn't let me. he said some people had trouble with differences because they had a hard time accepting themselves.

march 7, 11:19 p.m.

> **surfbudd3:** do u have a bf?
> **melicious:** y?

surfbudd3: u do

surfbudd3: does ur bf know that ur picking up guys in adopted kids chatroom? :)

melicious: im not picking up guys

surfbudd3: wheres your bf now?

surfbudd3: ah

surfbudd3: if u were my gf id treat u rite

melicious: he treats me right

surfbudd3: does he wear plaid flannel n go hunting?

melicious: flannel yes

melicious: hunting no

melicious: ur such a stereotyper

surfbudd3: ooh 5 syllable word

melicious: shut up

surfbudd3: do u love him?

melicious: y?

surfbudd3: if u dont love him y go out w/ him?

melicious: how do u know if u love someone til after u go out w/ them?

surfbudd3: u deserve better

melicious: do u have a gf?

surfbudd3: if i did i wouldnt be picking up girls in adopted kids chatroom

late march

i catch the flu and miss four days of school. my best friend lacey brings me homework and a little candle shaped like a bowl of chicken soup, which makes me laugh. during that time ben krupin calls exactly once to ask how i'm feeling, not that i'm in the mood to talk.

march 21, 12:08 a.m.

> **melicious:** i cant believe its snowing on the 1st day of spring
> **surfbudd3:** i thought the 1st day of spring was yesterday
> **melicious:** so its snowing on the 2nd day of spring
> **surfbudd3:** it was 65 and sunny here today :)
> **melicious:** u dont know how good u have it
> **surfbudd3:** u totally need 2 come 2 cali
> **melicious:** maybe

when i come back to school, i have two quizzes and a test to make up, so that's why i'm sitting in the spanish classroom after school on march 31. i don't think aiden sees me when he pops in, throws a piece of paper in the trash, and leaves. through the doorway, i see him continue down the hall, followed by this weird kid named jeremy greene. i'm in there by myself because the substitute spanish teacher, the one we have while mrs. gregg is on maternity leave, not only doesn't know spanish but also doesn't know not to leave kids alone in a room while they're taking a quiz. i start obsessing over what aiden might have thrown away. he's not the kind of kid that, if he's finished chewing his gum or whatever, he'd go out of his way to find a trash can. plus it didn't look like gum.

i leave the quiz face down on mrs. gregg's desk, and on my way out, i pick up the scrap of paper aiden threw away. it's a perfectly torn rectangle, and it says "Sheetz, St. Paul's Episco, Little Joe's," one underneath each other. a gas station, a (torn-off part of a) church, and isn't little joe's the truck stop off the interstate, on the way to carter springs? what's that about? i imagine aiden tearing up the paper and throwing it away, and the look on his face looks familiar. then i remember: it was the look on his face during the columbine assembly we had in fourth grade.

fourth grade current events: my parents subscribed to the stupid *new york times,* which didn't even have comics and which took five days to get to our house. a few times that year i lost points for bringing in articles that the teacher said weren't current enough. but the most important current event that year was columbine.

they told us about it at an assembly, and when we heard what happened, aiden whispered, "lucky kids. at least they don't have to go back to that shithole." i was so surprised he used that word at school, and wondering if anyone else heard, that i didn't even think about what he was saying. later, when i saw the pictures in the *new york times* of the kids who shot all those people in columbine, they had the same blank look on their face that aiden did. it was hard to sleep, thinking about those faces, and finally my mom took me to see the one licensed child psychologist in tillmon county, who told me there were plenty of grown-ups around to protect me, i just needed to trust them. she had me color pictures of helpful grown-ups, pictures from a workbook designed for much younger kids, and i felt ridiculous coloring generic pictures of parents, teachers, nurses, guidance counselors. what the hell does a guidance counselor look like, anyway? you could tell some of them were supposed to be black and some were supposed to be white, but nobody in the pictures was asian. like asian-americans were not helpful grown-ups.

in the doorway of the spanish room, my nails tear a hole through the scrap of paper. i think about looking in other trash cans, but i'm not nancy friggin drew, and i don't need aiden mcnalley asking why i'm collecting his garbage. in the absence of any helpful grown-ups, asian or otherwise, i throw the scrap of paper away in the big garbage can outside the school.

i make a bargain before i fall asleep: if i get at least a 98 on the spanish quiz (unlikely because of how much i was distracted), i will seriously consider moving to california.

april 1, 10:23 p.m.

melicious: i think maybe im coming 2 cali!
surfbudd3: lol

surfbudd3: april fools
melicious: 4 real! i got 102 on my spanish quiz!
surfbudd3: plenty of people speak english here ;)

april 2, 12:21 a.m.

melicious: would i go 2 ur school?
surfbudd3: maybe we could both get a ged
melicious: i dont want 2 b a dropout
surfbudd3: i heard the ged test is so easy
surfbudd3: we could pass it right now in our sleep
melicious: 4 real?
surfbudd3: y waste yrs of our lives in high school
surfbudd3: when we could just pass a test & move
on?

the truth is, i'm not in a big hurry for the world of work.
i work at a discount store called party!party!party!
where the main qualification is can you keep from laugh-
ing when people ask questions like, "do you think these
are easter bunnies or regular bunnies on this gift bag?"
my bosses like me, so i get away with things like not
mopping the floor when i'm on closing shift and refusing
to answer the phone by saying, "party!party!party! can i
help you, help you, help you?" — but in terms of doing
this full-time, i'm not over-anxious.

april 5, 1:49 a.m.

> **melicious**: have u ever been on a plane before?
> **surfbudd3**: of course
> **surfbudd3**: tons of times. u?
> **melicious**: just when i came here from china
> **surfbudd3**: r u serious? flyings awesome
> **surfbudd3**: like being part of the sky
> **surfbudd3**: part of the universe
> **surfbudd3**: okay, actually i only flew once 2 my
> aunts funeral
> **surfbudd3**: when i was 7

april 9, 12:07 a.m.

> **melicious**: how would someone under 18 live in cali?
> **melicious**: like $$?
> **surfbudd3**: eat a lot of macaroni
> **melicious**: u mean ramen
> **melicious**: if im going there 2 b more asian
> **surfbudd3**: lol

i've eaten chinese food maybe ten times in my life, mostly at this one place in flanders. i always get wonton soup and chicken with cashews, which is apparently not very chinese, but that's not my fault. when i left china, i didn't even have teeth yet. the one thing i do know is never to go to the sum ting special chinese restaurant in spruce valley, next to the laundromat on ninth

37

street. not only are they next to a laundromat, but they leave the door open all summer, letting flies in, and flies are gross. also i don't eat there because of the god-awful name, but if they didn't have flies, maybe i would get over that.

april 10, 11:49 p.m.

> **melicious:** how do i know ur not some 50 y/o pervert who gets kicks pretending 2 b a teenager?
> **surfbudd3:** if i was a 50 y/o prevert id tell u ;)
> **surfbudd3:** also a 50 y/o pervert wouldnt have a chem quiz tomorrow
> **melicious:** u should study or sleep or something
> **surfbudd3:** cant sleep
> **surfbudd3:** thinking about u coming here

april 12, 1:08 a.m.

> **melicious:** i packed a suitcase
> **surfbudd3:** cool
> **melicious:** im glad u live in southern cali cuz i didnt have room 4 sweaters
> **surfbudd3:** y?
> **melicious:** sweaters take up a lot of room
> **surfbudd3:** i mean what else did u bring?
> **melicious:** toothbrush books clothes pictures

surfbudd3: did u pack a picture of ur bf?

surfbudd3: its okay if u did

melicious: whats wierd is that i didnt think of packing one

surfbudd3: is it weird not telling ur parents ur coming?

melicious: if their even my parents

surfbudd3: ???

melicious: if there wasnt a difference being adopted there wouldnt b an adopted kids chatroom

melicious: every nite i look at my suitcase just as a reminder that i have options

surfbudd3: cali is like the land of options

surfbudd3: nothing personal against where u live

lacey has no idea about my plans. she thinks we tell each other everything, like we're the damn babysitters' club, with that one asian girl who's exactly like all her little white friends. but i haven't babysat since ninth grade, when a kid threw up all over me and his mom was nowhere to be found.

friday, april 21

at lunch, i try telling lacey about the apartment, but she doesn't like hearing about surfbuddy. she thinks it's wrong to spend so much time chatting with him when i'm supposedly dating ben krupin, even though ben krupin shows more affection to his stupid cat than he shows me. lacey thinks she's all grown up because her boyfriend's 28 and her dad's sick and whatever, but who wants to be all grown up?

april 21, 9:08 p.m.

> **surfbudd3:** they wont rent 2 minors
> **melicious:** what??
> **surfbudd3:** i went there but they said u have 2 b 18
> **melicious:** so say im 18
> **melicious:** its only a few months diff
> **surfbudd3:** how many months?
> **melicious:** 8 which is like nothing in the scheme of things
> **surfbudd3:** also the apt didnt look that nice
> **melicious:** ???
> **surfbudd3:** kinda grungy and beatup
> **melicious:** oh :(
> **surfbudd3:** i think if ur moving all the way across the country u should live somewhere nice
> **surfbudd3:** u should live in a palace

i'm desperate to get someplace warm and sunny, where people have seen an asian person sometime in their life. where i can be myself, whoever that is. friday night while my parents are downstairs watching some movie with subtitles, i take my dad's wallet out of the metal bowl on his dresser. i slide out the credit card and go online.

saturday, april 22, 1:58 a.m.

    melicious: 12:35 next saturday!!!
    surfbudd3: ???
    melicious: thats when u have 2 pick me up at the airport!!! don't b latelll
    surfbudd3: ur kidding
    melicious: nope decided itll be easier 2 find apt when im there
    surfbudd3: wow
    melicious: i have 2 wake up in the middle of the night 2 go 2 the airport which is like 4 hrs away in baltimore
    melicious: im thinking of asking lacey 2 drive me
    melicious: do u think she will even tho shell have to drive 4 hrs back by herself?
    surfbudd3: i didnt know u were that close 2 baltimore
    melicious: 4 hrs isnt exactly close but theres no real airports here

melicious: isnt that crazy? pissburg is closer but the flights were way more $$

melicious: my dad will go crazy enough when he sees his credit card bill even tho ill pay him back of course

surfbudd3: of course

melicious: u dont sound excited

melicious: cant u pick me up at that time? i mean its fine if i have 2 wait at the airport or something

melicious: i was just kidding about dont b late

surfbudd3: no the time is fine

melicious: so ill c u then?????!!!!! can u tell im excited????!!!!!

surfbudd3: um

melicious: what?

surfbudd3: i guess i shouldve told u b4

melicious: told me what??

surfbudd3: i didnt think youd buy the ticket

surfbudd3: if i knew youd buy the ticket id have told u b4 i swear

melicious: told me what??????

surfbudd3: esp knowing ur so close 2 baltimore

melicious: what the hell does baltimore have 2 do w/ anything???

surfbudd3: its kind of where i live

melicious: what do u mean kind of?

surfbudd3: ok its where i live

melicious: but u live in coconut beach

surfbudd3: no i knew a kid at camp from there he always talked about how great it is

melicious: ur freaking kidding me

surfbudd3: i wish

surfbudd3: i cant even offer 2 have him pick u up at the airport cuz he goes away 2 boarding school

melicious: i dont freaking believe this

surfbudd3: u know the worst part?

surfbudd3: ok maybe not the worst part

melicious: whatever

surfbudd3: saturday is my birthday i couldve finally met u on my birthday

melicious: ooh ur finally 16

surfbudd3: um

melicious: what?

surfbudd3: actually 15

melicious: go 2 hell

surfbudd3: i didnt think ud talk 2 me if u knew

melicious: i wouldve been better off

surfbudd3: maybe i really am 16, since no one is sure exactly when my birthday is

surfbudd3: r they sure about ur birthday?

melicious: goodnight

when i log off, i don't turn the computer off right away. the puffy clouds and sky on the screen are like the view out of an airplane window. i drag my suitcase out of the closet and unzip it, then i fling each item, one at a time, at the computer, out that imaginary airplane window, at

43

surfbuddy's head. i imagine my pajama bottoms landing around his neck and strangling him.

when lacey calls me at work saturday morning, i figure it's probably to apologize for not listening about the apartment. it's the weekend after easter, and we have to change the signs on all the baskets and plastic eggs and grass from twenty-five percent off to fifty percent off, plus the graduation stuff is coming in, and we have to squeeze that around mother's day. all those stuffed animals with caps and gowns remind me we're getting old. lacey hadn't wanted to hear about my apartment; maybe i didn't have time to talk to her right then either. the smiley face sticker on my cell phone is scratched and faded, but it stares up at me until i turn the phone off and shove it down to the bottom of my purse.

after work, i stay downtown, not wanting to face my parents or the house that it now feels like i will live in for all eternity. then i see lacey at the corner of main street and second, passed out and blood-soaked, with gloria hilliard's stupid dog taffy yapping around like it's a picnic. i ride in the ambulance with lacey to the hospital, and i'm there when she wakes up, but by then her dad is there too, so i leave. i'm not even mad that she didn't mention she was pregnant. at home, my parents left a note that they drove to pitts-burgh for an art exhibit, and i spend an hour forcing myself to stay away from the computer.

then, the weirdest thing: ben krupin arrives — with flowers — and apologizes for not being around more, an apology i only semi-believe, but still. when we finally do it, our first and only time together, i'm imagining the computer is on, webcam-enabled, and surfbuddy can see everything.

april 22, 8:21 p.m.

> **surfbudd3:** ill have my learners permit in 9 months
> **surfbudd3:** i could drive 2 c u
> **surfbudd3:** or we could drive 2 cali together
> **melicious:** what the hell do u know about cali?
> **surfbudd3:** or u could come 2 baltimore
> **surfbudd3:** nordstrom at towsontowne mall has narrow shoes
> **surfbudd3:** my sister & all her asian friends shop there
> **melicious:** people get killed by strangers they meet on the internet
> **surfbudd3:** not in nordstroms shoe dept

Hardware

Lacey

When you work in a hardware store, people assume all kinds of things about you. If you're a guy, they think you're into building stuff, like you take home tools at night to build birdhouses and fix lawn mowers in your spare time. People assume this about my dad and my Uncle Jack, which I guess is reasonable, and they used to assume it about my brother Jacob before he died. But the only thing I ever saw Jacob build was a dresser from Ikea, and when he finished it, two of the three drawer handles were attached on the inside.

If you're a girl who works in a hardware store, the things people assume are worse. They think you don't want to do anything in life, that you're just hanging out until graduation when you can quit and raise babies. Or they think you're stupid or a dyke. Working in other kinds of stores is different; people think you want a discount on the clothes or you get free food or something. But the reason I work at our family's hardware store is that the doctor in Carter Springs said my dad could have another heart attack if he didn't slow down, and we can't afford to hire more help since everyone started going to Home Depot. My dad says everything's fine, but he is like me and will always say everything's fine.

Anyway, I am not stupid, I am not a dyke, and I am definitely not planning to raise any babies, not after what my parents went through when Jacob died. My plan for as long as I can remember has been to go to college and become a nurse in a high-need specialty like geriatrics, so I can live wherever I want and always take care of myself.

I was so sure about not having kids that the first time I missed my period, in February, the obvious answer didn't even occur to me. I thought maybe it was the cold weather, or stress from the SATs, or even getting a new locker partner in P.E., because don't your cycles align in situations like that, and couldn't you miss a period while things are aligning? But in March, I started to wonder if I might be kidding myself because of P.E. being only twice a week. I never bothered with peeing on one of those sticks, but by April I was sure.

I didn't tell anyone, not even my family or my best friend Amelia. Definitely not my boyfriend Ed, who said one of the things he liked best about me was how I wasn't pressuring him about our future. If I loved him, it would have been a perfect excuse to get married and start a family, but I didn't love him and didn't want a family, so what was the point?

The morning Aiden and Jeremy and Jeremy's brother came to the store, I had found a spot of blood in my underwear. Could I have imagined the whole baby thing? But that morning I kept thinking about how there was this baby inside me, and maybe this baby was not fine. And in the middle of the morning — while I was on the phone with some rude lady who thought we should match Wal-Mart's price on lawn chairs — I felt this rush of blood, soaking through the panty liner and into the khaki pants I always wore to work. I tried to pretend maybe it was just a crazy period, maybe my body was back on track now and making up for lost time. But I remembered when my cousin Megan had a miscarriage when I was in sixth grade, and I heard her tell my mom that it felt like her heart or something was bleeding out. That was before Jacob died; nobody would have said that to my mom afterwards. Now my cousin's description sounded about right.

Which made no sense for someone who didn't want babies, but I couldn't help it. Once I had admitted a baby was already inside me, my view about babies got a little harder to figure out.

When Aiden and them came in, Aiden was wearing a leather jacket that made him look sexy in an old-fashioned way. Jeremy trailed around the store after Aiden, and Jeremy's brother followed both of them for a while and then got distracted. Finally they paid for their stuff — lighter fluid and two pairs of rubber gloves — and never noticed I was there, even when we talked about the barbecue they were planning. For all I mattered, they might as well have been talking to the giant cardboard light bulb that said "Lighten Up With Savings," a sign that had never made any sense to me.

Below the cardboard light bulb, taped to the wall behind the cash register, was a picture of me and Jacob and some of our cousins in Halloween costumes when we were kids. I was dressed as a caterpillar, and I was pouting because my mom made me wear my rain boots. Nobody meant to leave that picture in the store forever, but soon after that Halloween my cousin Landon stopped smiling for pictures, and then three years later Jacob died, so the stupid caterpillar picture became permanent. Probably I'd be sixty years old and still pouting in the stupid caterpillar costume — although who would be running the cash register at that point, I had no idea. Not me, that was for sure. But now I wondered: if I could be so wrong about never wanting babies, could I be wrong about all the rest too, college and moving away?

On Saturdays I unpacked the inventory that came in during the week, stocking the shelves and setting up displays, things my dad shouldn't do because of his heart. But as business got slower, there were fewer cartons to unpack and set up. I made it take as long as I could, because I liked the musty air and the old shelves crammed with odd-sized packages, things to keep around in case somebody needed one someday. That's how the store was, here in case somebody needed it someday. As our sales dropped month after month — spiking a little when people put up their gardens and when the first snow came, but not like before — I was sad for what it meant to my dad, but not entirely sad about what it might mean for me.

After Aiden and them left, the blood started coming harder and faster. I tied my sweatshirt around my waist so no one would see if it leaked through, but I was going through panty liners something crazy, so I finally went across the street to Foxtail's Pharmacy and bought a package of super-overnight maxipads. It was the first time anyone in my family had shopped in Foxtail's since the owners, the Peterschotts, refused to sign a petition against Home Depot a few years ago. The Main Street businesses used to stick together, but that petition was the beginning of each family for itself. Anyway, I didn't see any of the Peterschotts in Foxtail's, just a kid named Tyler who had a lot of pimples and seemed so nervous about working the cash register, like maybe it was his first day, that I wasn't even embarrassed about buying the pads.

After my cousin Megan had that miscarriage, she had two pregnancies that turned into my cousins Clayton and Avery. She bled both times and had to go on bed rest, so maybe however much I was bleeding was okay. A few times, my bleeding even slowed down. If I was still pregnant on Monday, I promised, I would stop kidding myself and get checked out, even if I had to go to the free clinic in Morgantown.

I stacked disposable cameras onto a cardboard display and tried to think about something other than babies and blood and hardware. And what I was going to tell my family, and my boy-friend Ed. So I thought about Aiden. There's probably nobody at Tillmon County High School less likely to help my future than Aiden McNalley, but he's made me laugh since first grade, when

Tim Conroy made fun of my name by calling me "Loosey Lacey," and Aiden bopped him with a lunch bag and M&Ms scattered everywhere.

Babies. Blood. Aiden. I couldn't believe I minded not being invited to his stupid barbecue. How could I even consider raising a baby when I still cared about high school barbecues? While I balanced the disposable cameras, I kept replaying Aiden's purchase over and over in my head. Then I began to wonder: if Aiden was having a barbecue, why did he need rubber gloves? Of course, it could have been an unrelated project, people buy all kinds of unrelated items at hardware stores, but finally I had to sit down in the gardening section and rest my head against a dusty bag of potting soil.

Babies. Blood. My other Aiden memory from elementary school was the day in fourth grade we had a surprise assembly in the middle of social studies. Aiden got in trouble at every assembly we'd ever had, and he had actually been banned from assemblies for a while after he unrolled a giant roll of toilet paper down the aisle during a choir concert. But they brought him in from the guidance office for this assembly, which should have told us something.

I was sitting next to Amelia, and when they brought Aiden in, our teacher made him sit on Amelia's other side. Then the principal told us how some kids in Colorado had killed twelve students and a teacher, and injured a bunch more, then killed themselves. The name of the school was Columbine, which was a flower I once saw a picture of when I was researching Columbus, Ohio, for a report and accidentally hit enter too soon.

I was thinking about that flower when I heard Aiden say under his breath, "Lucky kids. At least they don't have to go back to that shithole."

Amelia either hadn't heard or chose not to answer. No one else had heard.

I sent Aiden a silent answer: "I know what you mean." I didn't really, but I wanted to.

That week my aunt freaked out and took away all of my cousin Landon's guns: real guns he used for hunting with his father, plus water guns, army guys that were holding guns — she did this whole sweep while we were in school. I was at his house when he found out, and he was so mad he peed on the living room rug on purpose, and my aunt smacked him right in front of me.

I remember the dream I had, that Aiden went on a shooting rampage at South Branch Elementary. I woke up shivering, and I remember walking to Jacob's room, where he was still awake, typing a paper on the computer. He told me not to worry. He said sometimes people looked at his long hair tied back with a rubber band and thought he was someone to worry about, but he wasn't. Probably Aiden was nobody to worry about either. While Jacob finished his paper, I looked through his CD collection, mostly indie bands nobody in fourth grade had heard of. Then Jacob showed me secrets about this videogame he liked called Zelda, and I fell asleep on his floor, using his WVU sweat-shirt as a pillow.

That's where he wanted to go, WVU. When he got in that car accident, a couple of weeks after Columbine, he had already been accepted, and we were just waiting to hear about financial aid. But when the financial aid letter finally came, a month after he died, my mom threw it away without opening it. I dug through the trash, but my mom had also dumped out some old potato salad that someone brought for the funeral. The smell of the moldy potato salad made me want to throw up, so I never found out whether Jacob got enough financial aid to go to WVU.

Whenever someone mentioned Columbine, I always thought about Aiden at that assembly, and about falling asleep on Jacob's floor. I imagined kids from our school on TV, saying, "Aiden was a little weird, but I didn't think he'd do *this*." Of course he wouldn't. I remembered what Jacob had said, about how appearances could be deceiving.

■ ■ ■

When I stood up, I saw the disposable cameras were off-center on the display. I tried shifting them gradually, without knocking everything over. If Aiden and them were planning something dangerous, they wouldn't have bought the stuff at Miller's Hardware. They would have gone to Home Depot, because even if somebody's neighbor was there looking for lug nuts, and even if the

cashier was in their P.E. class, at Home Depot nobody would remember what they'd bought.

Don't assume things, Jacob would have said.

But what were those guys doing with lighter fluid and rubber
gloves? Jeremy Greene and his brother didn't seem dangerous.
The brother had some kind of problem and kids sometimes made
fun of him, but he seemed like a nice guy, not someone who
would burn the school down.

Was Aiden someone who would burn the school down?

Amelia didn't answer her cell. I figured she was at work, down
the street at Party!Party!Party! I called twice, three times.

A few weeks ago, our social studies teacher, Mr. Potempkist,
had been droning on and on about nothing when suddenly he
was talking about this woman named Kitty Genovese, who lived
in New York in the 1960s. She got raped in the courtyard of her
apartment complex, and then the guy left, came back, and mur-
dered her — and the whole time nobody helped, even though
like forty people must have seen what happened. Of course that
made me think about the drunk driver who killed my brother:
how many people saw this guy drinking and watched him get in
his car? How many of them could have saved Jacob's life? And
what if now was my chance; what if I was one of the people with
an apartment facing the courtyard, and I was the one who was
supposed to stop Aiden from doing something horrible?

When I stood up, I felt a gush of blood, and I knew I was losing my baby. If this baby had been born, I could have named

him after Jacob. Jake. My brother would have loved being an uncle.

The sheriff's office was at the end of Main Street, next to the Big Spruce Creamery. I could tell them about Aiden's weird purchase and get a hamburger for lunch. And a mint chocolate chip milkshake. It was the first time in months I was hungry.

I hung the "Back Soon!" sign in the door, locked up, and stepped outside. I remember thinking I could skip the sheriff's office, skip the milkshake, skip the hardware store and the last two months of school. I could skip town, skip stones, skip-to-my-lou, make a new life someplace like Morgantown and never be heard from again. I walked to the corner of Second Street and waited to cross. Gloria Hilliard was coming down the street with her mutt, Taffy, who she pretended was a Bichon Frise, and I remember hoping the light changed soon so I didn't have to smile and chat. I do enough smiling and chatting at the store. But I don't remember anything after that.

I don't remember passing out, or Gloria calling for help, or Taffy sniffing me in embarrassing places because of all the blood. (I heard about that later from Amelia, who had gotten off work at Party!Party!Party! and was on her way to visit me at the store.) I don't remember going to the hospital, and thank God I don't remember my dad coming, having him find out I was pregnant and not pregnant in the same conversation.

I had to have a sonogram to be sure nothing was left over in my uterus. That's what the nurse said, left over, like yesterday's meatloaf. Like I didn't just almost become a mom, and then not. Usually the sonogram technicians don't work weekends, so they had to page the one on call, who turned out to live in Pennsylvania. An hour later, she hobbled in on crutches. Skiing accident, she said, and I said that was too bad.

That night, before I fell asleep, I felt around on the top shelf of my closet, under my old bedspread and my Brownies uniform, until I pulled out the gray sweatshirt that said "WVU" in blue and gold letters. With no baby and soon, maybe, no store — maybe in a year and a half I'd bring the sweatshirt to college myself, although I wouldn't actually wear it. The sweatshirt didn't smell like Jacob anymore, but the soft fabric next to my cheek made me feel like I was in fourth grade again, up past my bedtime, safe on my big brother's floor.

Bottlecaps, Part One

Albert

Saturday morning I was in the dining room working on my bottlecap collection, and Mom told Jeremy if he wanted to go out, he had to take me with him.

People think I don't hear anything when I'm focused on my bottlecaps, but they're wrong. Right then I was checking if my 1941 Pepsi-Cola bottlecap was a genuine, mint-condition original, but it was hard without my magnifying glass. Jeremy had said don't carry that magnifying glass everywhere, he said something would happen to it at school, and something did. I got caught between two football guys who were skipping down Hallway 4 singing "reeeeee-tard, reeeeee-tard," and my backpack fell and got stepped on, and the magnifying glass broke.

It wasn't the end of the world because I had already memorized the details on my favorite bottlecaps, like the little blue bird on the Chirp soda cap and the expression on the clown's face on the Corky cap. Things like that stay in my memory, and I can look at them in my mind whenever I want.

Jeremy called, "Alpo, we're leaving in ten minutes!"

Ten minutes? That was too soon. I wished Jeremy would ditch me at least some of the time Mom made him take me out. Then I could sneak back home and work on my collection. But they all think I need somebody watching me, like I might eat paste again.

Ten minutes (nine, now). Was I wearing two shoes, two socks, pants, and a shirt? Check. Glasses? Check, or I wouldn't have been able to see my bottlecaps. Anything gooey on my teeth? Nope.

Suddenly a Nehi grape soda cap scooted across the table, knocking two other caps onto the rug. Then a Speed Stick whizzed by.

"Hey, do us a favor," Jeremy said.

I stuck my tongue out at him, but I put on the Speed Stick. Sometimes it was okay having a twin brother help me keep track of things.

■ ■ ■

We drove through town, filled up at Sheetz, and kept going way out Route 329 to Jeremy's friend Aiden's house. The mountains were half-hiding in fog. If I ever design a bottlecap, it will look like the Appalachian Mountains on a foggy day.

Aiden lived in a double-wide past the lake, but you can't see the lake from where he lives because of all the new houses. Aiden crushed out his cigarette when we pulled up, but he still stunk when he opened the door by my seat.

"Get in back," Jeremy told him.

I opened my window. Dad's a truck driver, due back that

afternoon from a nine-day Florida run, and I knew the car better not stink like smoke when he came home. In seventh grade, Jeremy and I both got busted for smoking. For punishment, we had to choose between smoking until we threw up or taking a beating, and Jeremy nudged me and we both took the beating. That was the only time I got in trouble with my brother. Even if I could think of something bad to do, my parents couldn't take away the car because I didn't drive, and if they grounded me, I would just work on my bottlecap collection, which was the same thing I did when I wasn't grounded.

The three of us drove back into town.

"Hey, Albert, we can trust you, right?" Aiden said. "You think we can trust him?"

I laughed a little, and Jeremy glanced away from the road and looked at me. Then he told Aiden in the rearview mirror, "Don't worry."

"Hey, Jeremy, where are we going?" I said. Sometimes when I talk people have trouble understanding me, like my words have to pass through an FBI sound garbler before they come out. Jeremy understands me better than anybody else, maybe because of knowing each other before we were born. But he didn't answer.

In downtown Spruce Valley, Jeremy parked across from Miller's Hardware. Miller's Hardware had rows and rows of tools, and little plastic and metal and wooden parts waiting to be made into something. Anything was possible at Miller's Hardware, especially if Lacey Miller was there.

Most girls didn't know how to talk to someone like me. Most girls either laughed or talked like I was a mental patient, slow and baby-talk. But when Lacey Miller rang me up, she'd say, "That'll be four fifty-eight," same as for anybody else.

While we waited to cross Main Street, Aiden asked Jeremy, "How come you brought him, anyway?"

Jeremy could have said, "My mom made me," which was true, but he said, "You got a problem?"

I was glad Jeremy threw me that Speed Stick, but if I knew we were coming to Miller's Hardware, I would have also clipped my fingernails and swiped some of his hair gel.

Aiden asked Jeremy, "How much does he know?"

A lot more than you think, I wanted to say. Not just about bottlecaps, either: I know about girls, and the Supreme Court, and the Civil War.

"Don't worry," Jeremy told him again. Which was when I worried.

Aiden asked, "Hey, Albert, do you know why we're here?"

I must have accidentally done the thinking face, where I think so hard that my chin scrunches up into my cheeks. My mom likes that face so much that sometimes when I'm doing homework in the dining room, she'll come and mess up my hair like I'm five years old. I hate the thinking face.

Aiden laughed. "Yeah, okay."

I wiped my palms on the front of my jeans, and we went inside.

■ ■ ■

In the store, Lacey was ringing someone up at the cash register, not smiling, just doing her job. Jeremy and Aiden walked around the store, picking up lighter fluid and two pairs of rubber gloves. I followed behind them. The narrow aisles were packed tight with anything a person could want.

"Are you guys doing a science fair project?" I asked. I remembered not to talk too loud, but I still sounded like I had cotton in my mouth.

Aiden said in a big, exaggerated voice, "Aw, gee, you're onto us!" in a way that I knew there was no science fair project.

He added, "But it's a top-secret science fair project. We don't want *any*body else to know, so you have to keep it a secret, okay? Can you do that?"

I wanted to tell him, I took karate, and I could flip you over my shoulder and leave you crying on those bags of charcoal. You see that patio table with the big umbrella? I could shove that umbrella —

But I didn't. I just gave him a look that told him how stupid I thought he was. Nobody wants to be called stupid by someone from Hallway 4.

Lacey's voice twirled over from the front of the store, like music.

"Yes, we have those," she was telling someone on the phone. "Twelve-eighty-seven, or two for twenty-four dollars. Uh huh. Well, ma'am, we stand behind the quality of our product a hundred percent. You ever have a problem and you just bring it back for a full refund. Uh huh. Well, ma'am, it's not up to me to make that decision, but — hello? Hello?"

I sat down on a patio chair. The metal armrest was cold and smooth, and I tapped my fingers against it a few times. Lacey's voice was clear and sweet, like a bird calling out in a special bird language. I could have listened to that voice forever.

"Come on, Albert." I followed Jeremy to where Aiden was standing with the shopping basket. We were the only customers in the store now, not like when I used to come with my dad in the olden days and we waited in long lines of people all buying the same stuff: charcoal or leaf bags or driveway salt, depending on what month it was.

When Aiden handed Lacey the lighter fluid, their hands touched. Her mouth made me think about strawberry ice cream.

"Hi," she said, looking at Aiden. But he didn't say "hi" back, just stared straight ahead at a fly-fishing display near the cash register.

"Hi," said Jeremy, and Lacey looked surprised.

"Are you having a barbecue or something?" Lacey asked, still looking at Aiden.

"Uh huh," Jeremy said, looking away.

I waited for them to invite her, now that their secret was out. I knew it wasn't a science fair project. It was one thing not to want me at their barbecue, but I couldn't imagine anyone not wanting Lacey.

When they didn't invite her, Lacey kind of flipped her hair to one side, except it wasn't quite long enough to flip.

"That'll be seventeen ninety-one," she said. Her mouth didn't look like strawberry ice cream anymore.

Aiden pulled three crumpled dollars out of his jeans pocket and then searched through his other pockets. Finally Jeremy put twenty dollars on top of Aiden's.

If she was ever going to talk to me, anything besides how

much my change was, it would have happened then. And it was ruined because Jeremy and his stupid friend hadn't invited her to the barbecue.

■ ■ ■

For the ride back to Aiden's house, I got in the back even though I didn't have to, so I could stare mean stares at the backs of their heads. And so if I did something stupid like cry, Jeremy and his friend wouldn't know.

Jeremy turned on the radio, and we heard Bob Binkley, who usually came on for the four o'clock request hour, welcoming us to KXZ Trivia Challenge Week. He played bing-bing-bing on his xylophone, and it was really him, too, not a studio effect. He came to our music class once and showed us.

But we didn't get to hear the thinking music he played while people answered questions, because Aiden jabbed the radio dial, turning it off.

■ ■ ■

After we brought Aiden home, I told Jeremy, "It's okay if you don't want to invite me to your barbecue." We were on Route 329, the part before the auto parts stores and Food Fair. The windows were open a crack, and I had to shout a little over the rush of air.

Jeremy closed the windows.

"There's no barbecue," he said. He kept his eyes on the road. Jeremy was a good driver.

"But Aiden said — "

"There's no barbecue."

I wished we could go back and tell Lacey. Maybe I could tell her at school, find her in the cafeteria and explain. But as nice as she was, she still would not want to talk to me in the cafeteria.

I asked, "Then why did Aiden need lighter fluid?"

Jeremy stared straight ahead. He had never been in a wreck, or even gotten a speeding ticket.

"Just don't worry about it," he said. "Pretend you didn't see what he bought."

"I saw it," I said. "He bought a 32-ounce jug of Kingsford lighter fluid."

Jeremy didn't answer.

"But I did see," I said again.

Jeremy sighed. "Probably nobody will ask," he said. "But if they do, can you just do that for me? Pretend you don't know what's going on?"

Jeremy gripped the steering wheel so his knuckles made sharp little angles. If anybody else had asked me that, I would have said no way. I hate when people assume I don't know what's going on. I know more than people think.

But to help Jeremy, I said okay.

Earrings

Rob

1. First Earring

NYC, eighth-grade wannabe,
me and Mitch in
Mitch's kitchen
after school:
he just got accepted,
I just got rejected
by the School for Performing Arts,
my earlobe numb where
Mitch had held the ice cube.

Jaycee Speigelmire calls him with an invite
to a swim party at her summer house:
a pool dug into a hill,
a van ride to Connecticut on milky leather seats.

I pretend the same message
is waiting for me at home.

I saw Jaycee's apartment once
for the cast party
after sixth-grade *Guys and Dolls*
(in which I was Sky Masterson and Mitch was only
Nicely-Nicely, I'm just saying).
The bookshelves in Jaycee's living room
slid all the way into the wall,
shhhhhhoop.
Another whole wall was window,
which Mitch said must confuse the hell out of pigeons.
If that was Jaycee's city place,
I could only imagine the Connecticut place.
And imagine is what you have to do
when you're not invited.

Mitch had a
yellow paperback book
that said how to pierce ears.
Numbing my earlobe took forever.
Later I found that book
in a used bookstore I went to after school
so I didn't have to go home.

In the book the person getting pierced
held her own ice cube,
and I wondered:
did Mitch not read carefully,
or did he change things
slightly
on purpose?

2. Second Earring

In the West Village
after fighting with my boyfriend,
who was nineteen
and worked at that bookstore.

"Where the hell is Lake Albright?" he said.
And "Who the hell moves to Appalachia?"
That would be me.
It had to do with my father's job
and how some of his numbers were
very occasionally
off
in a direction that let my mom update her jewelry
every season

and paid my tuition
at Dalton.

We're lucky, said my mom.
Lucky-lucky-lucky,
Lucky ducks, Lucky Charms, lucky me.
My lucky father ratted out
his not-so-lucky boss,
Murray,
who cracked me up when I was little
by asking if I was driving yet
(which I finally am,
even if it's just a permit).
By being a rat and paying a fine,
my father avoided
jail.
Murray got eighteen months.
Maybe it would have been worth
eighteen months
not to move to Tillmon County.

Who the hell moves to Appalachia?
I ran out of the coffee shop,
abandoning my avocado melt and my boyfriend,
across the street to Earring Emporium.

Ping.
But if I thought a second earring
would make my life symmetrical
I was wrong.

3. Third Earring

Jaycee has Connecticut, but
my family has Aunt Lucy,
who lives with her partner near Pittsburgh
and spends August at Lake Albright, in
Tillmon County.

Aunt Lucy said
the house sits empty
and my mom could freelance
while my dad worked in Pittsburgh
during the week.
Aunt Lucy said
it would do me good
to get away.
Aunt Lucy thinks gay people
should live in Appalachia
and stop putting holes in our ears.

Maybe gay people
outside the city
have to try harder
to prove how normal they are.

It did not do me good to get away,
not here,
where they think the new season means
how many deer you can kill,
not how faded are this year's jeans.

Ben Krupin, my lab partner,
wore flannel shirts crazy big
and jeans faded not on purpose,
but from ignoring them,
which is the worst thing you can do to jeans.
His white sneakers made his size eleven feet look bigger.
But I liked how he walked,
not caring what anyone thought (I thought).
Like one of these damn mountains (it seemed).
Like Mitch.
I was wrong.

My parents left for Murray's trial.
They thought seventeen was a good age

to start shielding me from drama,
so I was alone in the house
with wide wood floors and a big open loft
and no curtains on the windows
so you could look at the stars,
which I have to admit are better here
than in the Hayden Planetarium.
The loft has a built-in bench
where you can listen to rain
and look at a pile of magazines
you brought from New York,
in case it took a while
for your subscriptions to find you
(which it did).

My parents stayed the whole weekend.
I kept almost telling Ben they were going,
but I was afraid he'd ask why.
Finally I invented a sick relative,
invited Ben to the big empty house.
But even as he said okay
(his eyes said yesyesomigodyes)
I knew he wouldn't come.

Just in case, I changed clothes three times,
first wearing all black,
then jeans and a plaid shirt, but they were New York jeans
(tight and professionally faded, way too expensive
but worth it for that fit)
and New York plaid
(orange background and wavy turquoise lines —
don't hunters wear orange? —
but this shirt was soft, like suede, and dry-clean only,
and hunters do not wear turquoise).
Finally I wore what I wore
every week with Ben:
a sweater that made my eyes look deeper blue, and
cargo pants with lots of pockets
that I filled so Ben could guess
what was in them:
Big Red gum, and magazine pictures
of things he'd look good in
if he started caring about clothes.
Also funny condoms I ordered online
from the West Village,
happy faces, and flavors like
cotton candy.

I waited for Ben for two hours
even though I knew
before I got there
he wouldn't come.
Then I came home
(to this pretend-home)
and slept.

In an envelope on the fridge
under a Monet water lilies magnet,
my mom left money for pizza.
Ben liked pepperoni
so I ordered the opposite:
black olives, green olives, and capers
(as if I needed salt because I was crying or something,
which I wasn't).
The girl said, "Olives and what?"
and when I told her she said,
"I don't think we have those."
The pizza came with black olives
and anchovies, to punish me.

To keep from calling Ben,
I stuffed my keys
in my cargo pants

and walked.
New Yorkers walk everywhere,
but people here take their cars
to buy a freaking candy bar.
Hiking up the falls with Ben
was the only place I walked anymore,
so the place in Tillmon County least like New York
was most like New York
that way.

What if I had gone back
for a jacket?
Or waited to order the pizza?
Would the pizza guy have burned up?
He had pimples the exact size and shape of
capers.

What if Ben had come over?
We would have eaten
pepperoni pizza
on the deck,
used good dishes
and maybe drunk some of my parents' good wine
or, knowing Ben, A&W in wineglasses
while the sun set

behind the mountains.
We would have kissed on the deck,
then gone inside.

The satin sheets were not on the bed in his honor —
I always slept with satin sheets —
but I would have enjoyed his reaction.
That's where we would have been,
satin sheets and warm skin,
pepperoni and
organic green tea body wash
(which was in the bathroom in his honor,
not that he would have noticed).
By the time we smelled smoke,
it would have been too late.
We would have died together:
smiling,
but dead.
By being an asshole,
he saved my life.

I walked halfway around the lake,
to the side without houses.
A train roared past,
and I threw pebbles in the lake.

One for every hike,
every touch,
every hair on the back of his knuckles
that made me think of the Jolly Green Giant.
A pebble for Big Red gum
and cotton candy kisses.
The crickets laughed at me.

One pebble extra hard,
for when he said I made him want to quote country music.
My life was a country music song:
my father lied in an audit so I moved to the sticks
and got my heart broken by a hick.
When that pebble hit,
something shattered,
and the sound was so perfect,
I didn't realize at first:
pebbles don't break
lakes.

Boom!
Across the lake,
flashes of light.
I walked then jogged to the house
in my idiot patent-leather shoes

caked with mud and grass.
I heard sirens and thought briefly
of parades:
Apple Glory, Winter Wonderland, and Daffodil Days.
I think if one of the County commissioners peed straight
someone would have a parade.

The street was blocked with fire trucks.
I told a fireman, "I live here,"
and he looked me up and down,
like anyone could see I don't belong here.
It was probably the shoes.

The fireman let me
use his cell phone
while all my ring tones
burned inside.
It took two hours
and three fire companies,
and when they were done
the house looked like it had died.

Someone burned down my house
in Nowheresville.
My clothes were no more.

I'd have to get jeans at Ogleby's Outdoor Shop
or, God forbid, Wal-Mart.
I'd look like whoever burned my house down.
After I reached my parents, the fireman asked,
"You got a place to wait?"
He offered to open the firehouse,
like he was inviting me to a pancake supper.
I said no thanks because it was Saturday night
and the firemen wanted to go home,
and what would I do at the firehouse for five hours?

So I drove to the falls
and rolled down the window
and played with the perfect threadbare spot
on my perfect cargo pants.
I thought about Ben
and Mitch
and Bookstore Boy
and whoever set the house
on fire.
I almost died.
And Ben didn't want me.
Those two facts jumbled together.
It was easier being mad at Ben.
A thread broke on the pants.

In the future
I wouldn't ever say
I had lived here.
On the map
in my social studies book
I'd color over every mountain
in dark, dark pen
until they all disappeared,
like Ben.
But first I'd drive to Carter Springs Mall,
get a new hole in my left ear
and a new silver stud
and Thai food from that place in the food court
that is so not Thai.

Blink-blink, blink-blink,
a car waited to turn in
to the falls.
It looked a lot like Ben's car.
I would've been sure
if all that damn smoke didn't bother my allergies,
making my eyes tear up.
I floored it and aimed toward the highway.
Blink.

Most Valuable Brass

Jeremy

You could say everything started on the last day of all-state music camp, when, for the first time since I was eligible, I didn't win the award for Most Valuable Brass Player. The person who won, a freshman (a freshman!) named Lindsey, lived almost in Pennsylvania, where she wouldn't even have been eligible for this all-state music camp. But that part wasn't, technically, anyone's fault.

On the second day of music camp, the freshman named Lindsey was in line ahead of me at dinner, and she did not take either the pork or the fish entree.

I asked her, "Are you a vegetarian or something?"

She said, "Yeah."

Since I knew it was her first time at music camp, I told her, "You have to make sure and get protein. The third day is when you start needing a lot of stamina."

I wouldn't have minded if someone talked to me about protein my first year at music camp, so I added, "If you want, I could get you a peanut butter ice cream later, at the canteen. Peanut butter is an excellent source of protein. A lot of people don't know that."

Lindsey said no thanks and turned away. I had thought that away from home, away from my brother, where I could play trumpet with the best of them, that would be my best chance for a girl like Lindsey to talk to me. Now I knew I had no chance. And Lindsey had to rub it in by winning the award.

I came home from music camp determined that my junior year would count for something.

■ ■ ■

But maybe everything really started when I got contact lenses for my birthday in September. I was sick of my glasses fogging up after early-morning band practices, and my parents finally gave in, even though it was one more thing, like marching band and my driver's license, that made me different from Albert.

On the first day of school, while our English teacher was passing out vocabulary assessments, Aiden McNalley asked me, "You new?"

I looked at him like I've seen people look at Albert.

I said, "Aiden, I've been in your class since middle school."

"Did you used to have glasses?"

I nodded.

"Oh," he said. "Can I copy from you?"

Then I knew I was dealing with an idiot. "It's a vocabulary assessment. To see what we know. It doesn't matter what score you get."

"So you won't care if I copy. Thanks."

After that, Aiden talked to me sometimes, in class and in the cafeteria. I always ate lunch with my brother so Albert didn't have to sit alone. But now Aiden said "hey" as he walked past, and a couple of times he even sat down.

If I had thought the contact lenses would improve my chances at making friends, I did not have Aiden McNalley in mind. I had no more interest in being friends with Aiden than with the sad guppies that swam back and forth in the tank outside the main office, never going anywhere. But when you help somebody out like I did, you feel obligated to help them in the future, like you want to prove it wasn't stupid, helping them the first time. So that's how Aiden and I got to be, if not friends exactly, then the kind of people other people thought were friends.

■ ■ ■

Aiden had been saved during the summer, and he sometimes said I should get saved too, but I always said no thanks. I'm undecided about the whole God thing, because why would any God take two twins and mess one up for no reason? But Aiden wasn't big on undecided.

He also wasn't big on church, it turned out, choosing to venture out all by his own saved self. In December, Aiden decided his mission was to rid our school of the scourge that was preventing the Second Coming. I looked up "scourge," and it meant something that causes great trouble or misfortune. At first I thought he was joking. How could the Second Coming be stopped by anything in Tillmon County? If Jesus was that powerful, why couldn't he just Come if he wanted?

"What God hates," Aiden explained, "is anything unnatural. Like cannibalism or incest or two guys together. Anything unnatural."

I wondered whether he thought Albert was "unnatural," but I kept my mouth shut.

■ ■ ■

And so, really, everything began with the list. Aiden made a list of everything unnatural in Tillmon County, which included KXZ, for playing pornographic music, and the Quik-Mart, for its magazine selection. When I asked him why Wal-Mart wasn't on his list, how that was so "natural," he didn't talk to me for two days. But he added Wal-Mart to the list, right after the Tillmon County Health Department, which told girls where they could get abortions. Back then, Aiden didn't seem much further gone than plenty of other people, not much crazier than the vegetarian who won Most Valuable Brass player at music camp.

■ ■ ■

Then on March 31, the day before April Fool's Day, Aiden tore up the list. After I finished band practice and Aiden finished detention, we were smoking outside the front entrance to the school. Thanks to marching band, I no longer had to put up with the school bus like Albert did, but I still had to wait around like a first-grader for my mom to pick me up, and I had to remember to crush out my cigarette before she came.

With no warning, Aiden tore the list out of his notebook and ripped it into thirty-two identical-sized pieces. Then he went inside and started walking, throwing the papers into thirty-two separate trash cans, saying that way no one would rummage through the trash and tape the pieces back together. This should have been proof enough to me that Aiden was crazy, because even if someone did find his master list in the trash can, what did it prove about anything?

But I hurried behind him, hopeful. The weather had been in the 40s and sunny, and I was going to ace my solo in the statewide Battle of the Bands. And now Aiden was getting rid of the list.

"It's superficial," he explained. "I've been trying to purge this county's magazines and music while disgusting things are happening all around us."

"There's cannibalism all around us?"

He looked at me.

"Probably," he said. "But at least the sickos who practice that don't throw it in our faces."

The way he said that, I knew what disgusting thing he meant. And after seeing Rob Sullivan in his tight jeans walk across the parking lot like he was on Rollerblades, I knew who Aiden thought was throwing things in our faces. It's not like I think we need more gay people on the planet or whatever, because then how would the species reproduce? And I guess there's something a little weird about a guy deciding to be with another guy when there are so many beautiful girls in the world. But I also think people are the way they are, whether it's because of God or genetics or something else. Blaming people for being gay is like blaming Albert for being Albert.

"What are you going to do?" My throat was dry, and I glanced at every water fountain we passed.

"I can't discuss it with someone who's not going to help," he said.

I thought about Rob Sullivan and the Second Coming, my fear of saying yes and my even bigger fear of saying no. And my resolution back at music camp, that I would do something that mattered.

When I whispered, "I'll help," I wasn't even sure at first if I said it out loud or only in my head.

■ ■ ■

Arson: the crime of maliciously, voluntarily, and willfully setting fire to somebody else's building, buildings, or other property. First-degree arson can get a person ten years in jail, but
Aiden said I wouldn't get that long because it was my first offense. Most people who commit arson have already done lots
of other stuff, like drugs.

Even so, I tried not to read too much on the Internet. Maybe
this was the biggest thing going on in Aiden's life, but our band
teacher, Mr. Macomb, was getting ready to retire and was running us extra hard to get ready for his final Battle of the Bands.

■ ■ ■

When the night came, on April 22, we hid in the woods near
Rob Sullivan's house on Sky Valley Drive until it got dark.
Aiden shushed me for swatting a mosquito, and I almost swat-
ted him next. It was cold and damp, and we had forgotten the
rubber gloves, which had seemed stupid to me anyway. Did
Aiden think someone would get our fingerprints off branches?

When it got dark enough, Aiden said, "Come on." We
climbed up the path, Aiden carrying the lighter fluid, and me
behind him with two matchbooks we'd found at the last minute under the floor mat of the truck, sticky with orange soda.

The house was dark except for one little light on the second
floor, which, if it was there to fool potential burglars or arson-
ists, was not doing a very good job. The house had big, funny
angles, like the rooms were built separately and hammered
together at the end. Aiden had watched the houses go up when
we were kids, and I knew plenty of people who had worked on
those construction crews, hauling in special lumber to lots that
had been cleared of boring old Tillmon County trees. My uncle
Bill told my dad he was crazy not to join up: four dollars an

hour more than my dad got as a trucker, plus no overnights. But my dad refused to trust the big construction companies, and eventually Tillmon Citizens for Smart Growth made a fuss that stopped the construction, which is why the big, patched-together houses are only on one side of the lake.

Anyway, Aiden knew the houses pretty well, and he motioned me over below the deck.

I handed him a matchbook and he struck a match, but — nothing. He tried two or three more, but still nothing happened. The other matchbook didn't work either. The orange soda must have soaked all of the matches. It was like the opposite of the burning bush.

I heard a sound then, or imagined I did, and we got out of there. The truck smelled musty, nauseating, and I left the windows down even though it was cold. Marching band builds up a lot of stamina for weather.

Driving Aiden home, I thought: I didn't even know who else lived in that house. What if Rob Sullivan had an old grandmother who listened to the radio in the dark and couldn't hear the smoke detector because the radio was too loud? A little old grandmother didn't deserve to die. And Rob himself — maybe he had a cold and went to bed early, or was texting away with just his cell phone glowing, too dim to be seen outside. And whether he was texting Bible verses or if it was love notes to other guys, he didn't deserve to die. In all of Aiden's planning and scheming, we had never talked about the possibility that somebody could die.

But somebody could, whether at Rob's house, whenever Aiden made it back there, or somewhere else — because this one fire might not be enough for Aiden. Maybe the almost-fire was a warning: for all of Aiden's talk about being saved, maybe I was supposed to save Tillmon County from Aiden.

So after I dropped him off, instead of going home, I parked illegally on Main Street and ran into the sheriff's office. I was freezing and sweating at the same time, like the cold air and the fire were battling it out inside me.

I had never been in the main part of the sheriff's office, just the multipurpose room where volunteers helped to organize crates of donated food every year for the Christmas drive. The main building was quiet and dingy. The building seemed deserted, but I wasn't about to leave without telling someone about Aiden. If I had to, I'd go next door to the jail. Louis Riley would be there, drunk and half asleep like he had been since Spruce Valley got founded, practically, but he'd listen to what I had to say.

But down at the end of the fourth hallway, a door was half-open. When I opened it the rest of the way, the woman behind the counter looked up at me like I had caught her doing something wrong, although she seemed to be doing her job, typing things into a computer. She looked like an elementary school attendance aide, slightly fat, kind and no-nonsense at the same time. I walked through.

"I — there's a — somebody's gotta — " I stammered.

"Slow down." A sign on the desk said her name was Jocelyn Fitzmiller.

There was a girl in the waiting room too, someone I knew from school even though we'd never talked. She changed the spelling of her name so often — Kate, Cate, Kait, Cayte — that nobody noticed anymore, or cared.

Jocelyn said, "This is my sister. You don't mind if she's here, do you?"

"It's okay. Hi, Cait," I said, suddenly remembering how she spelled her name this year. She had won an essay contest about what she would do if she were governor, and they had framed her winning essay in the lobby near the band room. I had never read the essay, but I could picture how her name was spelled under the title, C-A-I-T.

"Hi," she said.

Jocelyn asked me, "Can I get you a chair, sweetie? Or a Coke?" Like I was a second-grader who'd just gotten hurt on the playground. Which was pretty close to how I felt.

"No thanks," I said, meaning the Coke, but then I didn't know how to say okay to the chair. So I stood near the counter, just too far to rest my hands on it or kick at the bottom of it with my shoe. Jocelyn was behind the counter on a high-up swively chair, and Cait was on the folding chair in the waiting area, looking at a poster in Spanish about what to do if someone is choking. Which was kind of crazy, because as far as I knew the only person in Tillmon County who spoke Spanish was Mrs. Gregg, the Spanish teacher, and how likely was it that she would happen to be at the sheriff's office when someone was choking?

■ ■ ■

Finally, Jocelyn asked, "So, how can I help you?"

I tried to sound calmer than I looked.

"I — there's this guy I know," I said. "I think he's a little crazy. Like maybe dangerous."

"Hmm," Jocelyn said. "Why do you say that?"

Then I told her about Aiden and his list. I told her everything I could remember, because I didn't know what was important or where things went out of control. I'd kept Aiden's craziness inside my brain for so long that it felt like my craziness.

Cait had closed her eyes, but her forehead was wrinkled,

like she was focused. I wondered if the focus needed to win essay contests was anything like the focus needed for marching band. She was wearing jeans and a hooded sweatshirt.

Would Jocelyn call someone? Would I be stuck here all night for questioning? I should have eaten before coming in, at least grabbed a hamburger from the Big Spruce Creamery, even if they were overpriced and the perky freshman waitresses would see me there by myself on a Saturday night. With everything I knew about protein, it was stupid of me to come out without dinner to start with, let alone make an extra stop at the sheriff's office.

But Jocelyn looked like she had heard everything before, and she wasn't rushing to call anyone.

I hadn't mentioned the fire yet — I was thinking I would, that she'd need to know about this not-quite-fire to accurately conclude that Aiden was a crazy person — but I took too long explaining about the list, trying to remember everything on it. I was telling Jocelyn about Blockbuster Video, how I wasn't sure if Aiden meant the whole chain or just the one in Tillmon County, when the scanner crackled on the countertop.

Jocelyn saw me look at it and said, "Don't worry, honey, probably another cow loose on 329."

I smiled a little. At least twice this spring traffic got tied up while everyone waited for a cow to cross the highway.

On the scanner, voices called numbers back and forth. Lots of people had their own police scanners, always turned on, and they had all the codes memorized. It was like a soap opera for math teachers, where all the drama happened in numbers.

I did hear "Sky Valley Drive," and for a second I wondered if Aiden could have gone back after I dropped him off, if he could have set the fire after all. But that was stupid. He wouldn't have had time.

■ ■ ■

The next couple of minutes had more action than I had ever heard on a scanner. The number I kept hearing was four-seven-seven, which sounded random enough, like a locker number. But Cait was looking at her sister, and Jocelyn had that look grown-ups get when they don't want you to know they're more scared than you are.

"Whoa," said Cait. "Arson."

"Sounds like," said Jocelyn. "But who knows?"

My stomach turned. I thought about Rob Sullivan's imaginary old grandmother, how if she burned to death, it was my fault. I wished I were religious so I could pray for Rob not to have a grandmother. And for no one to have been home.

I couldn't just turn and run out of the sheriff's office without looking suspicious, so I said, "Uh, it looks like it's not a good time right now."

"Hmm," Jocelyn said, "well, things might get crazy in a few minutes, but if you want to file a report — "

"I'll think about it," I said. "I'll definitely think about it."

■ ■ ■

I drove to the bottom of our road for a smoke, which was what I did when I needed to think. Before I met Aiden, smoking was the only thing in my life that didn't somehow help either Albert or my trumpet-playing, and the one way I knew I was still a normal teenager. I pretended to my family that I didn't smoke, and my parents pretended not to know. Albert was the only one in our family who was what he seemed to be.

But as I lit my cigarette, I stared at the lighter, like it was left in my pocket by alien forces. Had I really forgotten it was there? When Aiden discovered that his lighter was used up, I had patted the side pockets of my windbreaker, where my lighter should have been, but I should have patted the inside pocket too, where it sometimes went, especially if I was afraid of it falling out in the hall closet at home. It would have taken just one extra pat, and I might have even felt it without that pat, might have felt it just in checking the left side pocket.

But even without the lighter, Aiden and I had burned down a house. When we left, there was just a pile of dead leaves and branches, but a little while later the house burned down. That spark must have been there all along, must have gathered strength under that pile until finally, when nobody was looking, it took over. Like Aiden: whatever was in him probably smoldered all these years under the piles of crap people threw on him. And when he was done smoldering, somebody's house burned down.

And maybe killed someone. I hadn't heard anyone on the scanner talk about anyone being home, but maybe they said it in code. What was the code for Rob Sullivan and his imaginary grandmother coughing and choking to fight their way out of a burning building?

I was crushing out my cigarette on the gravelly road when a voice called out behind me.

"Jeremy!" said our neighbor, Mr. Jacoby, shining a flashlight in my direction. He worked at the FedEx center in Carter Springs, scanning packages in the middle of the night, so his days and nights were mixed up.

"Cow got loose?" I said, trying to seem like everything was normal. The Jacobys' mailbox had a smiling cow named Elsie glued on front, and kids liked to break off the legs and udder.

"No sir!" Mr. Jacoby said, as if he were hoping someone would ask that question. "I finally got the law looking out for whoever's been abusing Elsie. And looky what I got in the meantime!"

I shuffled over. Up close, I could see the black patches on Elsie were covered in sticky tar.

"Anyone tries to rip Elsie apart now, they'll be in for a surprise."

"But won't the tar dry?" I asked.

"And I'll be out with another coat quicker than you can say jack," he said. "I got three gallons this afternoon, had to drive up to Home Depot because Miller's had a sign out about a family emergency. You know anything about that?"

"No." I paused, wondering what had happened at the hardware store after we left. "You really called the police about your mailbox?"

"Should've done it years ago. Hey, did your brother find you okay?"

I stopped. "What?"

"About eight o'clock. Just before I found Elsie's leg and decided on the Great Solution. Albert came looking for you, so I told him which way you and your friend drove off to."

I stared. When Aiden and I left the lake, there was no fire, but a short time later there was. And Mr. Jacoby had seen where Aiden and I went and sent Albert along to follow.

Could Albert have seen — or, more than seen — could Albert have . . . ? No. Albert could not have, would not have set Rob Sullivan's house on fire.

"I gotta go," I said. For the second time that night, I made a point of exiting calmly, swallowing my panic until no one was around.

Whether Albert set the fire was one thing; whether people thought he did was something else. Mr. Jacoby was nobody, a man who devoted his life to the cow on his mailbox. But he saw me and Aiden drive toward the fire, and he saw Albert follow. And when he called the police about the stupid cow — it wasn't a stretch to imagine them asking if he'd seen anybody around, and wouldn't he naturally mention me and Albert just because he liked us so much and wanted to clarify that Elsie was already defiled before we ever came by? If he only knew what that would make people assume. People were always looking for reasons to assume things about Albert.

■ ■ ■

Aiden had quit making payments on his cell phone, not that I would have known what to say even if I could have talked to him. I got ready for bed quietly, mostly, until I accidentally banged my knee on the dresser and yelled, "Shit!" I waited for Albert to sit up from under his lump of blankets. "Wha-what?" he'd say, like he'd just dozed off for a second and was afraid he'd missed something. But he didn't wake up. I thought about giving his blankets a shove, to make sure he was really under there, but what good would it do to know for sure? Probably he was real tired from his day, which started with seeing Lacey Miller at the hardware store. I was real tired too.

During the night, I woke up once to a sound that might or might not have been Albert coming into our room. But by Sunday morning it seemed like the end of a very long dream.

■ ■ ■

Sunday Aiden came over early, around eight-thirty. His face looked stretched and puckered, like it had gone through a defective washing machine at Glo, Baby, Glo!

"You heard?" he said.

"Do you know for sure no one was home?"

"Relax about that," Aiden said. "But I gotta tell you — I'm eighteen, man. When I was a kid, I did kindergarten twice."

While I waited for him to go on, birds called to each other and someone fired up a rototiller. He came over to tell me how old he was? That's how naïve I was, and Aiden knew it.

"Man, I'm an adult. I could get sent away over this."

I asked without thinking, "So why'd you do it?"

I waited for Aiden to say he didn't do it, that he had figured out Albert was somehow involved. But he kicked at a pebble.

"I didn't think it would really happen. Nothing else I planned ever went like I thought it would, you know?"

I did know. I hadn't believed the fire would happen either.

"So now what?" I said.

Aiden shoved his hands in his jacket pockets and looked past me, toward the Jacobys' house. "Can you say it was your idea?" He paused. "You know I wouldn't ask if I had any other choice."

I struggled (like Albert struggles?) to get what Aiden was saying.

"It won't matter for you. But I'm eighteen, man, and I've already got a record. Just a DUI and riding with someone who had pot, stupid stuff, but it adds up with these people."

"You're crazy," I said, but I wondered: if Aiden didn't know Albert was involved in the fire, maybe nobody else had to find out. I didn't say okay, exactly, I just stood there silently and let Aiden think what he wanted.

"You're okay, man," he said.

I stood on the porch and watched him leave. If I told what really happened, it wouldn't take long for people to ask about Albert. Whether he set the fire or not, it would give people a reason to put him away someplace. They'd look at each other

94

and say, "See? I knew something like this would happen." If Aiden thought Tillmon County wanted to get rid of him, then he didn't know what it was like being Albert.

This could ruin Albert's life forever, but Aiden was right, it wouldn't matter that much for me. I could say I did it. Me, yeah, I just felt like setting a fire that night. What else could anyone ask? And if the sheriff's office had my name at all, it was because I volunteered three years in a row for the station's Christmas drive. Was the law extra-forgiving of people who helped with the Christmas drive?

■ ■ ■

Sunday was the one night *Jeopardy!* wasn't on, even in reruns, so when Officer Lind came to our house, Albert and I were playing checkers on the living room floor. When I saw the headlights, I tried to act casual, kinging Albert's piece. But Albert was standing up, opening the door before Officer Lind even rang the doorbell.

"Hi, Officer Lind," he said. He knew Officer Lind from those "Officer Friendly" programs at school. He dressed the same for school assemblies as he did to come to our house: khaki pants and a light blue shirt that strained over his stomach.

"Hi, Albert," he said.

I gripped a checker so tightly it left an impression on my finger.

"Officer Lind!" my mom said in the voice that meant she was surprised to see someone but didn't want to be rude. (Like, "Mrs. Jacoby, what a treat, of *course* we're up already," fumbling with her bathrobe.)

"Sorry to bother you folks," Officer Lind said, stepping inside. "I hope I'm not interrupting supper."

"No, we've eaten," my mom said. "But maybe I could get you some pie?"

"Sounds delicious, but I'm afraid I can't," said Officer Lind, putting his thumbs through his belt loops.

My heart thumped like I was at an audition.

When my dad came downstairs, I saw that he had splashed cold water on his face, trying not to seem like he had been asleep for the past five hours since he got back from his Florida run. We all sat at the dining room table, and my mom served Officer Lind a big wedge of chocolate cream pie and a steaming mug of coffee, apologizing that it was instant.

"I shouldn't," said Officer Lind, patting the part of his stomach that hung over his belt. "I gotta answer to my wife and to a couple of fancy doctors in Carter Springs." But he picked up a fork and started on the pie.

"So, what do we owe this visit to?" my dad asked.

"Well," said Officer Lind, dabbing at his mouth with a napkin, "like I said, I hate to bother you folks. But you might have heard talk about a disturbance last night by the lake?"

My parents glanced at each other. The paper wouldn't be out until Tuesday, and no one had had the radio on. And we hadn't gone to church since my grandmother died, when Albert and I were in third grade.

"No, sir," said my dad. "I don't believe we've heard that sort of talk."

Officer Lind cleared his throat. He looked at us around the table and then spoke to my dad.

"A house on Sky Valley Drive burned down last night," he said.

"Hmmph," said my dad. "That's too bad, but I can't say I'm surprised."

Officer Lind and my mom both looked at him sharply.

"Why's that?" said Officer Lind. He had a notebook, closed, on the table in front of him.

"Those builders," said my dad. "They know the people that buy those houses don't know about electric, and they only live there a week at a time. Wouldn't surprise me if they cut corners on the electric so they could buy their own vacation homes in Florida."

"Hmm," said Officer Lind, relaxing. "Well, some folks was living in this one, but nobody was home at the time."

"Thank God for that," said my mom.

I felt tension drain out of my shoulders.

"Yes, ma'am," said Officer Lind. "Thank the good Lord for that."

"More pie?" said my mom.

"Better not." Officer Lind patted his stomach. "Bev says one more pound and she's gonna start tagging along on my house calls."

The adults laughed, and for a minute I almost believed Officer Lind came to our house to eat pie and share the news. We listened to the clink of Officer Lind's coffee cup, the tap-tap of Albert's shoe against the table leg, and the whistle of the 8:05 coal train.

Officer Lind cleared his throat again.

"Something I hate to trouble you with," he said. "But there's talk about Jeremy might know one of the boys that might know about the fire."

"Jeremy?!" my mom said, in a way that hurt my feelings, a way somebody might say, "Albert?!"

I glanced at everyone and shrugged.

"Sometimes when we're talking to young folks," Officer Lind said, "it helps if we're not in the same room as their families. Just helps them remember better sometimes."

My dad said, "Well, there's the den; you're free to use it, of course, but I don't think it's going to help Jeremy remember something he wasn't involved in." He added, "Just excuse the tax papers out on the desk in there," like he wanted to point out what law-abiding, tax-paying citizens we were.

So Officer Lind sat in the swivel chair by the computer, and I sat on the old plaid sofa that folded out to a bed. My parents' diplomas from Tillmon County High School hung on the wall above the computer, my dad's at a slight angle.

"Well," said Officer Lind. "You're not under oath and you're not under arrest. I want you to just relax and tell me what you know, so we can help the people who need help." He was doodling in his notebook, circles that occasionally turned into little faces. His finger bulged over the top of his wedding band.

I nodded, but nothing I could say would undo the fire. So what difference would it make if I started it, or if Aiden did, or if it was the flute section of the All-State Band?

I took a breath and said, "I did it."

I stopped hearing the crickets outside, and my family moving around. My brain was full of static, like a police scanner. Officer Lind stopped doodling.

When I didn't say anything else, he said, "Tell me what you mean by that, Jeremy."

"Well," I said, "I didn't think it was right, what that kid was doing. Not just being homosexual, but making sure everyone knew it."

Officer Lind wrinkled up his eyebrows and ran his finger over the spiral part of his notebook.

"And what kid is that?" he asked.

"Rob Sullivan. The kid who lives in the house. Or lived there."

98

"Mmm," said Officer Lind. "Is there anything else you want to tell me about how the fire got started?"

It bugged me that he didn't say, "how you started the fire," like he didn't quite believe me.

"No, thanks," I said.

Officer Lind sighed and stood up, crossing his hands in front of his belly like the pie might try to push its way out.

"Most times someone fibs to the police," he said, "it's to claim they didn't do whatever it is they did. You don't see it so much the other way around."

"But I'm not — "

"You'll get your chance," he interrupted. "I'll take you to the station to fill out the paperwork. But just saying you done something don't mean you done it, Jeremy. I thought you knew that by now."

My parents were still at the dining room table when Officer Lind said he was taking me in to fill out some paperwork, and if it wasn't too much bother, could one of them follow behind us to drive me home?

My mother stood up, holding a foil-wrapped package. "I wrapped up some pie for Mrs. Lind," she said. She was like a lone clarinetist who keeps playing the music when everyone else is in chaos, so it comes out looking like she's the crazy one.

"Glenda, for God's sake, he's arresting our son," my father said.

"Just a formality," Officer Lind said. "Whole thing won't take more than twenty minutes. But I'm sorry about having you drive into town."

He was right: it was only seventeen minutes from when we arrived at the station until he took my picture and my fingerprints and released me to my dad, who didn't say a word during the drive home.

Riding through the darkness, I tried to see if I felt different now that I had been arrested, if this was finally the thing I needed to do that mattered. But instead of feeling free, like I had done what I had to and could get back to my life, I felt something tighten in my stomach, like I was the one who ate too much pie. As soon as we got home, I ran out of the car, and I made it to the bathroom just in time to vomit all over the floor.

Whether Tillmon County needed saving or not, I was not the man for the job.

Bottlecaps, Part Two

Albert

"Where are you going?" I asked Jeremy while he put on his socks. We were in our room, during that nothing-time before dinner Saturday night, the day of our trip to Miller's Hardware.

"Nowhere," he said.

"Then why are you putting on socks?"

Jeremy said, "People say 'nowhere' when they don't want to say where they're going."

"Are you meeting a girl?"

"Don't you have bottlecaps to organize?"

"I did it this morning. Remember, when you said it was time to get Aiden? Remember?"

"Yeah." Jeremy smeared gel on his hair.

"Does it have to do with Aiden? Does where you're going have to do with our trip this morning?"

He didn't answer, and I followed him to the front door, where he put on his shoes and jacket.

"Are you going to a barbecue?" I asked.

"Yeah, that's it, I'm going to a barbecue."

"Because first you said there was a barbecue, and then you said there wasn't, and now there is again."

"If you want to believe I'm going to a barbecue, then believe that. If you want to believe it's something else, it's something else. But I gotta go." He picked up his backpack and yelled goodbye to Mom. Then he went outside and started up the truck.

I've lost things before, like how I don't have that magnifying glass anymore, so I know what it feels like. I liked that magnifying glass, and even if I get another one someday, it won't be the same. It might be better in some ways and worse in others, but it will be different. Lately I have started to wonder if losing a person is anything like losing a magnifying glass.

■ ■ ■

Jeremy was usually the person I asked questions to, but I couldn't this time, because it was him that I was worried about losing. I listened to the truck drive off, and I fiddled with a bottlecap in my pocket. Something wasn't right with Jeremy, and maybe he needed my help. Sometimes a twin is the only one who can save his twin — if he can find him.

"Albert, dinner's ready!" my mom called at the worst possible time. Because I didn't know what else to do, and because I was hungry, I gobbled three chicken tacos as fast as I could. It helped that my mom didn't expect me to say much at meals.

As soon as I was done, I ran upstairs and opened my top dresser drawer, where on the left-hand side, behind a blue cardboard box of my very best and favorite bottlecaps, I kept my emergency preparedness kit. It was in a hard plastic case with my initials scratched into it. I clipped a fanny pouch around my waist and slid the emergency preparedness kit inside. This was my first time using it in an actual emergency.

I sat down on the bed and tapped the plastic ends of my shoelaces together. Then I stopped. My mom was still downstairs in the kitchen, cleaning up from our dinner.

That was a whole new problem. Now I couldn't get to the front door without passing directly in front of her. Jeremy could walk out the door and drive anywhere he wanted, just like Jeremy could wear contact lenses and play in the marching band, but I couldn't. Sometimes things like that got me mad, and sometimes they got me sad, but other times they just made me think harder until I thought of something else.

I shifted my sneaker back and forth from one hand to the other and looked through one of the little holes where the lace went through. Like a window. Like the window in the upstairs hallway, which is the only one in our house a person can fit through. I saw Jeremy do it once, when we accidentally locked ourselves outside.

I was almost too big to fit. The time we locked ourselves outside was a lot of years ago. The ledge dug into my stomach, but finally I pushed forward onto the roof of the carport. I slid down a metal pole, scraping my hands against the chipped paint.

Then what? I was cold in my jeans and my Pittsburgh Pirates T-shirt. It had been a long time since I was outside at night. Crickets called to each other. I bet if a cricket went missing, its brothers would have no trouble finding it.

The truck was gone, but my mom's Taurus was still there, and for a second I wondered, could I drive it to where Jeremy was? Driving looked easy enough when other people did it, but some things were harder than they looked. Plus I didn't have keys. So I ran down our road, toward Route 329. Wherever Jeremy went, he had to take Route 329 to get there.

Even if Jeremy never said thank you for this, it was okay because I would still know I had started to repay my brother. And I would be the kind of person other people could count on, not someone who always depended on everyone else.

The day the football guys knocked the magnifying glass out of my hand, I said, "Hey, that's my magnifying glass," and they pushed me against a locker. I got rescued by Jeremy shouting, "Hey!" which got the attention of the pregnant Spanish teacher, who said, "What do you gentlemen think you're doing?" and sent them all to detention. But after that the football guys made it worse for all of us on Hallway 4, which made people mad at me. Rescuing people could be tricky.

■ ■ ■

At the end of the road, our neighbor, Mr. Jacoby, was outside with a flashlight, looking in the grass near his Elsie the cow mailbox.

"Hi, Albert," he called when he saw me, like it was a normal night for everyone.

"Hi," I said, slowing down.

"Saw your brother earlier," he said.

"Yeah. I'm gonna go catch up to him."

"He forgot something, huh?" said Mr. Jacoby, nodding. "I'm always forgetting things when I rush around like that too. Where was he off to, anyway? I wondered when he didn't turn up 329."

My brain worked hard to get what Mr. Jacoby was saying. Didn't turn up 329? I was afraid to ask him for a repeat. If Jeremy hadn't turned up 329, then he had turned left at the bottom of the road. And if he did that, the only place that led was a back entrance to Lake Albright State Park.

"Albert?" Mr. Jacoby was saying. "It's okay. I just wondered because he was in such a hurry."

"He was going to the lake," I blurted out. "I gotta go, bye!"

"Bye, Albert," said Mr. Jacoby. "If you see a wooden cow leg on your way, save it for me, will you?"

"Okay," I called.

I ran faster to make up for lost time. The coal train was coming through town. As I ran, my feet hit the road in a rhythm with the train: "Gotta save Jeremy. Gotta save Jeremy." It wasn't like an even-steven thing, like I had to save him because he saved my butt so many times. This was deeper down, like having to sort my bottlecaps. Like an animal that doesn't think about whether someone deserves to be rescued, it just sniffs the air a couple of times and goes to where its owner is lying in a ditch.

But my sense of smell is not extra-developed like an animal's, so I couldn't just sniff the air to find Jeremy.

The crickets were louder, crickets and little bugs and who knows what that hide during the day and come out at night when they think no one is looking. I followed the path around the lake and turned up a hill that led to one of the houses. I don't know if I heard something or smelled something, or if I just knew because of me and Jeremy being twins. But I got up near the top of the path and waited behind some trees. Then, over the crickets' noise, I heard:

"Idiot." (Aiden's voice.)

"I could have told you matches won't light after they've been soaked in orange soda. That stuff will eat right through your teeth. I'm surprised the match is still here." (Jeremy, of course.)

"Shut up."

If Jeremy had kept going with Boy Scouts, he'd have known what to do with matches that wouldn't light, but he quit because of me, because I was scared to sleep in a tent when our Cub Scout pack advanced from Bears to Webelos.

I wanted to yell out that I had a lighter in my emergency preparedness kit, but I knew I shouldn't yell, even if I wasn't sure why. To keep from yelling, I tapped a twig against a tree.

Jeremy stopped. "Did you hear something?"

Aiden stopped. "No."

"I definitely heard something," Jeremy said.

"Think the squirrels will report us?"

I thought Jeremy would look at me, say something like, "Albert, what are you doing here?" but he didn't. For the first time in my life, even my brother didn't know where I was.

"Well, I heard something," Jeremy said. "That's it for me."

Aiden must have decided that was it for him too, because the two of them disappeared around the side of the house.

Did rescuing Jeremy mean finishing what he had started? I could finish it no problem: one click, and everything would fall into place, like finding the last bottlecap from a set. I could let Jeremy think he had done it himself, like he always tried to do for me.

I knew Jeremy always had good reasons for things, so I figured this fire was something important. And if Jeremy ever found out I had been there and didn't help — well, I'm a lot of things, but I'm not someone who lets his brother down. I finally had a turn at being the big brother, the one who was older by two minutes and forty-one seconds. I might never have a chance like that again.

I took a deep breath and looked at my hands to make sure they weren't shaking. They weren't, but I had some dirt under my nails.

My heart thumped while I opened my emergency preparedness kit and tried not to look at the empty slot where the magnifying glass used to be. At least I hadn't brought the whole kit to school, so I still had the Swiss Army knife, the Phillips-head screwdriver, and the nail file. Then, where there used to be a corkscrew, I had the lighter Jeremy and I used when we tried smoking. It seemed like a good thing to save, like in an emergency I might need a lighter more than a corkscrew.

In my mind, I heard Jeremy saying, "You can do it, Albert. Don't listen to anyone who says you can't." When I came out from behind the tree, I looked both ways, like someone crossing a street. Then I ran to where Jeremy and Aiden had been, in the space under the house. It was cool and dark, and covered with soft leaves. If Jeremy didn't need my help, I could have sat there a long time. This cool, dark place could swallow me up for as long as I needed to be calm.

I slid the lighter out of its pouch, then I flipped through my mental video library to the day we tried smoking, and I zoomed in close on Jeremy lighting the cigarette. Finally I bit down on my tongue, put on my most serious thinking face, and flicked the lighter like Jeremy had. A spark popped out and hopped around the leaves, then paused for a second before bursting into flames. Seeing it start so fast like that made me know it was the right thing to do, and I found a spot under the trees where I could watch. The flames looked a little like the waves on the 1941 Pepsi-Cola bottlecap.

I watched the fire for a while, and then: crack. The basement window split, a long spidery crack at first, then all the pieces flew out in a pop that made me step back several steps. I told myself not to be scared and made myself remember that I was helping Jeremy. That relaxed me a little, like he was there with me. Then another pop. Like the first few Fourth of July fireworks, which were usually on July 2 because the town could get them for cheaper. I always loved fireworks, like the boom-boom-boom could hide whatever was in my head and let me disappear into the sound.

This sound was relaxing like that, like all the pressure burst through the glass and escaped through the cracks. Once a substitute teacher brought our class to an assembly about why you should never cut yourself on purpose with glass. The substitute teacher didn't know that kids from

Hallway 4 didn't go to assemblies. It was okay until one kid threw a chair in the aisle and another kid went home and cut herself, on purpose, with a broken Scotch bottle. She lost a lot of blood, and it could have been serious if her mom didn't always look for the Scotch first thing after work.

I stepped further into the woods, where everything was quiet. When I heard crickets again, I put the lighter back in my emergency preparedness kit and watched the fire, then the fire trucks, until there were so many people it was hard to see. Then I went home the same way I came.

Gulf

Cait

In the waiting area at the sheriff's office, the chairs
have faded from tangerine to dirty school bus in the
years I've spent sitting on them. Which is nine years,
starting in second grade when I decided I'd rather
spend the time between school and dinner watching my
sister Jocelyn work than facing who knows what at
home. For nine years after school I'd read or help my
sister staple or file papers.

There used to be four of those chairs, but a leg broke
off one, the vinyl cushion ripped on another one, and
one got "borrowed" by Officer Montgomery to hold papers in his office. But as long as there's one chair left,
that's where I'll go.

People get used to seeing me there and forget to shut
up in front of me. Jocelyn once said, "You could write a
book with all the stuff you overhear in here."

I guess I've always been a little over-imaginative.
Like, I could be in line at Food Fair with my nephews,

picking up buy-one-get-one-free macaroni and cheese off the floor, and convince myself I'm not their aunt, I'm their au pair from someplace fancy in Europe. And even though nobody would believe that for a second, it doesn't matter, because I believe it, and that gives me the strength to ignore the rude looks and not clobber the boys when they start sword-fighting with the green rubber bars that divide people's groceries on the conveyor belt. Imagining I'm an au pair is like wearing a secret mask.

But this I did not imagine: I was at the sheriff's office the night of the fire, when Jeremy Greene ran in like a crazy person and told my sister about his friend on a mission to get Tillmon County ready for Jesus, like He had booked His summer vacation here, and we still hadn't washed the sheets and towels from the last guest. It could have been a coincidence, Jeremy coming in that night and making a fast exit when news about the fire came in on the scanner. But writers know you can't put too much coincidence in a story, or people will think it's not true.

■ ■ ■

Jocelyn works in the Office of Tax Services, and she stays late sometimes to use the computer for this class she's taking, even though she's technically not supposed to. She could get in trouble because the computers have lots of top-secret, highly confidential tax information, like whether Miller's Hardware is or is not behind on its eleven-cent tax bill. Just an example I'm making up. I keep telling Jocelyn not to mess with the computers, because if she lost her job, then what would she do? She's got pretty much the best job you can hope for without a degree — but she says this is the kind of rule-breaking that doesn't hurt anybody, and if she gets through these classes and gets her degree, then she can upgrade her stupid computer at home, and maybe by then her part of the county will have high-speed Internet.

For the longest time that night, nobody came into or out of the building. Tillmon County is not exactly a place where something happens every minute. Or every decade. And when something does happen, it's always one of the same few things: DUI, drugs, domestic dispute, or assault — the main difference between domestic dispute and assault being that one happens in somebody's house, and the other happens in a bar after they leave. Really it's a matter of when people can afford to go out and get drunk, and when they have to do it at home.

Jocelyn is friends with the dispatcher who usually works Saturday nights. He doesn't say anything about her hanging around the sheriff's office, and she doesn't say anything about him drinking in the alley. Which, I realized later, is where he must have been when Jeremy ran in, looking for someone, and instead of anyone useful, found us.

"Hello?" he called. He looked like he had just finished running a marathon he hadn't trained for and might pass out any second.

"Is there someone — "

Jocelyn slid over to the counter. She's thirty-one but still more stylish and graceful than I'll ever be. You'd never know she has three kids.

"Hi, sweetie, how can I help you?"

"I — there's somebody's — "

"You wanna sit?"

Jeremy glanced at me sitting in the only chair.

"I'm fine," he said, but I knew he was wondering whether to leave. I thought about getting up and taking a walk, but my ankle was hurting more than I wanted my sister to see. I had twisted it to avoid ramming into a coat rack when my stepfather pushed me after he saw my cell phone bill. The crazy part was, the bill was just the regular monthly charges, for the phone my mom made me get so she could always find me. I'm the last person on earth who would waste money on fancy ring tones or whatever. But I didn't want to walk and get Jocelyn all worried about my home life if I didn't have to. I wished I had a magazine, any magazine, to look busy. I could look real busy with *Field and Stream*. But no one donates their old magazines to the sheriff's office.

Jeremy stood where he was, and Jocelyn said, "Why don't you tell me all about it?"

"Well," Jeremy said, glancing at me, "I just — I thought I should tell someone about this friend of mine."

"And why's that, sweetie?" Jocelyn was so used to her job that practically nothing fazed her anymore. That was my goal, to be someone nothing fazed anymore. She leaned against the counter, and her Wal-Mart rhinestone bracelet sparkled.

"Well, see, it started with, well — "

"Take your time," said Jocelyn. "Can I get you a Coke?"

For years, Jocelyn had been giving me Cokes from this red and white cooler, and I used to think it was something the sheriff's office did for free, a service for people to help them relax and say what they needed to say. Then one day I saw her stick a dollar bill inside an envelope taped to the back of the cooler, and I realized she had been buying my Cokes all along. The next week, I stole ten dollars from my stepfather's pants that he had flung over a kitchen chair, and I put the money in Jocelyn's coat while she was in the bathroom. It was a start. And it was only fair that my stepfather pay, since he was the reason I'd been coming there for nine years.

I was glad when Jeremy said no to the Coke.

"See, this kid I know is a little obsessed. But lots of people are obsessed, it doesn't mean they're dangerous."

"Of course not," Jocelyn said.

"He had this list of things that were — well, don't laugh, but things that were preventing the Second Coming."

"Mmm, mm-hmm," said Jocelyn. She nodded and pressed her fingertips together, in a way that said she was really listening.

"But it got a little . . . out of control."

Jeremy looked scared, which surprised me at first, but then I remembered he had that brother who was retarded or whatever. That had to make a guy more sensitive.

But before Jeremy could say what happened, the scanner started going crazy with people talking about the fire. And somewhere in the confusion, Jeremy left.

■ ■ ■

"Do you really think it's arson?" I asked Jocelyn later.

"Wouldn't surprise me," she said, "with how this county's going these days."

"Do you know how old that makes you sound?"

"Maybe I'm old," Jocelyn said. "But before they put those millionaire houses by the lake, did you ever hear about any fires that weren't from faulty electric?"

"That house in Mount Jenkins got hit by lightning two years ago."

"You know what I mean."

■ ■ ■

Tom Gillienheid is technically not even my stepfather yet, even though he's lived with us for thirteen years. But just lately they've been talking about making it official and getting married this summer, which I think is ludicrous. Tom is like sixty, and he's got two grown-up sons and an ex-wife in Kentucky. Sober, he didn't give me a lot of reasons to hate him: he tried to help me with homework when I was little (before he figured out that I didn't need help), or he'd offer to drive me places without complaining about how much gas we were using. We liked a lot of the same places, actually, like the used book section of the Salvation Army store in Carter Springs, and McDonald's for caramel sundaes. But whenever we went somewhere alone, I imagined people looking at us and assuming he was my father, with no way to correct them. And my mom was always too tired to come, so mostly we stayed home.

And then he'd start drinking. Also he'd start drinking when my mom had final exams and was out studying a few nights in a row, and he'd start drinking when she was between semesters and was home so much they got on each other's nerves. And my stepfather, or whatever you want to call him, was a whole different person when he was drinking. That's why Jocelyn and I called him Jekyllnheid: the alcohol was a potion that turned him from someone sort of normal to someone you just didn't know.

Maybe that's why I'm the only kid at Tillmon County High School who has never knowingly had a sip of alcohol. Well, partly because I don't get invited to parties — people have to know you exist to invite you to a party — but partly because of my fear that if I take one sip, I won't be able to stop, and my life will spiral out of control. Once I bought the wrong kind of cough syrup ("DM" instead of "CF," or maybe the other way around), and I took it for four days before I realized the first ingredient was alcohol. I was terrified after that, checking and double-checking myself for signs of addiction. Crazy, I know.

My real dad was going to make a better life for us when he came home from the Gulf. He and my mom had been making plans for getting us out of Tillmon County when Saddam Hussein invaded Kuwait. My dad had been a National Guardsman, doing what they said in the ads, and he was going to cash in, go to college, and get a job in Morgantown or Wheeling as a computer engineer. By now, we'd probably have two mansions: one to live in wherever we ended up, plus a vacation house on Sky Valley Drive so we could enjoy the mountains when we wanted to and remember where we came from.

But of course nothing happened the way it was supposed to. National Guardsmen aren't supposed to get killed in foreign countries.

■ ■ ■

Jocelyn's car started on the first try, and she eased out of the alley behind the sheriff's office. I moved a Happy Meal toy out from under my leg.

Jocelyn was singing along with Carrie Underwood, *"I ain't in Checotah anymore,"* and tapping her butterfly-painted fingernails on the steering wheel when she drove past Stenton Road, where she should have turned to take me home.

"JoJo?"

"Mmm? *Catchin' crappie fish, I ain't in Checotah anymore."*

"You missed the turn."

"Yeah, well, if you don't mind the couch tonight, we'll move you in with Madison tomorrow."

"Move me in? You don't have to — "

"Are you kidding? It'll break her little heart if you'd rather sleep on the couch than stay with her. The only thing is if her music drives you crazy. You might be singing Elmo during algebra."

"Elmo's fine," I said. Probably better than Checotah, I thought, and I had finished algebra three years ago. But how long was Jocelyn planning on me staying there? I mean, Tom wasn't — it wasn't like I was in one of those situations where I needed a whole different place to live. Escaping during the day was one thing — didn't every

118

teenager sometimes need an escape? But moving out was different.

"You don't have to let me stay with you," I said.

"Shut up," Jocelyn said, but she was smiling, and thank God the radio went to commercial.

Once you leave Spruce Valley, driving through Tillmon County at night is like driving into a dream. In the daytime, the road is kind of held in place by the mountains, but at night there aren't any lights for the forty miles to the interstate, so the road could be anywhere, headed off the edge of the earth.

"I didn't ask if you wanted to stop for clothes or anything," my sister said when we were almost to the interstate and it was too late to drive back.

"I'll ask Mom to send stuff, or I'll go when he's not home."

"Not that you've been planning this."

At night, the interstate is mostly filled with trucks, the biggest ones that do the longest hauls. In the dark you can't see the car seats in Jocelyn's car, so the truck drivers probably thought we were carefree single girls, cruising around on a Saturday night.

"Do you think Jeremy set that fire?" I asked her. "Don't you think it's weird how he came in all crazy about his friend and then left when he did?"

"Look, I barely know what I know. And you don't know anything. I could get fired bringing you around to listen to people's confidential conversations."

"But he said — "

"Katydid, I'm just an admin. Whatever anybody tells me counts as much as if they told it to Madison."

"So you *do* think it's weird."

■ ■ ■

Jocelyn and I weren't always close, mostly because of our fourteen-year age difference. When our dad died, I was just one year old and she was fifteen, so when our mom went back to work, Jocelyn spent a lot of time babysitting me instead of hanging out with her friends. My mom got a receptionist job in the admissions office at Tillmon Community College, which let her take two classes a year for free, and after about a million years she got her so-called two-year degree. Jocelyn got to take classes for free too, but in her second class she met her husband, Paul, and they had Cameron right away, so she got a little sidetracked, but she's back now, in the same million-year plan my mom did. I'll probably go there too, but I'm taking as many classes as they let me, so I can hurry up and get my four-year degree. For that I'll go to Boston, maybe, or California. Wherever I get a scholarship.

Once I asked my mom why there were so many years between Jocelyn and me. I was eight then, and my mom was folding laundry and cursing our stupid dryer that still didn't work right, even after her friend

Patty's husband, who was supposed to be a certified repairman, had looked at it twice, and what was a person supposed to do, string underwear across the living room?

Anyway, I thought asking might take my mom's mind off her problems, get her thinking about when Jocelyn and I were babies. But my mom looked at me like even the question made her tired.

"Katie," she said (that was the year I was Katie — more like half a year, because I never liked that name). "Having one little girl kept me busy enough those first fourteen years."

"And it kept Daddy busy, too," I said. "Right?"

"Right," my mom said, barely pausing, such a little non-pause that it hardly even counted. But I always thought of it when I thought of the age difference between me and Jocelyn. And I knew I must have been an accident; I'm not stupid. But in health class we learned that 49 percent of pregnancies were unplanned, so I had a lot of company. And weren't most good things in life accidents? Like my parents meeting at the Spruce Valley Diner, during the two months my mom worked there, on a day she wasn't even working her regular shift. If my mom hadn't been covering for Patty, my parents wouldn't have met, and Jocelyn and I wouldn't have been born. I liked to think of myself as a stroke of good luck.

■ ■ ■

Monday morning, Jocelyn was mushing up a sweet potato for the baby, whose hair was already smeared with orange globs. Her kitchen had stuff piled everywhere: newspapers, cereal boxes, pink plastic dishes decorated with bears. You could look at the mess and know that nobody would ever go hungry in this kitchen.

Jocelyn looked a lot like my mom: arched eyebrows that were always asking a question, and ears that didn't curl all the way over up top. I don't look like them. My dad was usually the photographer, so there weren't many pictures of him mixed in with the ones of Mom and Jocelyn in the backyard or in the kitchen, squishing hamburger patties. In the few pictures we do have, I don't look much like him either. But I figure I am probably like him in other ways, like maybe how we walk, or our sense of humor.

Jocelyn looked up. "Do you need a ride to school?"

"No, I'll catch the bus."

"I'll drive you to the stop, then," she said. "Open wide for the choo-choo!"

Madison grinned and lunged for the sweet potato, which Jocelyn swooped into her mouth.

In a couple of months, Madison was going to be the "flower baby" at Mom's wedding, and Cameron and Kyle would be ring bearers. Whether I moved back home or stayed in the land of the flying sweet potato, Jekyllnheid was about to become a permanent part of my life.

Sometimes I ask questions at not exactly the most appropriate times. Like when I said to Jocelyn just then, "Do you ever wonder what would have happened if Daddy had come home from Iraq?"

Jocelyn looked at me, at the baby, at the glob of sweet potato that had escaped onto the floor.

She ignored me and yelled, "Cameron, Kyle, get yourselves down here for breakfast!"

"You know, what life would be like, if we would have gotten out of Tillmon County."

"If we had gotten out of Tillmon County, I wouldn't have met Paul, and my kids wouldn't exist."

"Well, you know what I mean. It's just so random, Daddy's unit getting called up — "

"His unit didn't get called up," Jocelyn said under her breath. Madison reached for the spoon, and the two of them guided the sweet potato toward her mouth.

"What are you talking about?"

"He volunteered. No, Maddy, we don't throw cups."

"You're crazy." I picked up Madison's sippy cup.

"Suit yourself," she said.

"Eh! Eh!" said Madison, watching her cup.

I set it back on her tray.

"Why would he volunteer? Nobody even cared about that war. And he was going to get a good computer job and buy a big house — "

Jocelyn shrugged.

"Believe what you want," she said. "I'm just saying

Jake Jensen, Ronnie Gregg, Jeff Owenbraun — they were all in Daddy's unit, and none of them went to Iraq."

"Well, but, why would he volunteer? There must have been some misunderstanding."

"That's one way to think of it. Kyle! Cameron! Down here, now!"

Madison pulled her bib up over her face and smiled like she had just won the lottery. I wet a dishtowel and started wiping her down.

"What are you saying?"

"I'm saying — you have this fantasy, where we were, like, this close to the perfect life. We were nowhere near the perfect life."

"But if he had come home — "

"If he had come back from Iraq, he wouldn't have come home," Jocelyn said. She hoisted Madison out of the high chair and onto her hip. "Boys! Five minutes 'til we leave for the bus stop!"

"What are you talking about? Where would he have gone?"

Jocelyn shrugged.

"Back to his apartment on Ninth Street, I guess. He lived there for, like, a year before he went away."

Our dad had an apartment? I knew the apartments on Ninth Street, above the Glo, Baby, Glo! laundromat and Sum Ting Special Chinese restaurant. I had been inside one once, to work on a project with a girl in fifth

124

grade. It smelled like cooking oil and industrial-strength laundry detergent, two smells that you would think would cancel each other out, but they didn't.

"A year?"

"Yeah, eighth grade was great," Jocelyn said. "I'm covered in acne, there's a baby crying all the time, Mom's a wreck, and I'm spending weekends on my dad's couch listening to people do laundry at four a.m."

"I was crying all the time?"

"This isn't about you."

"Well, but, Mom and Dad couldn't have hated each other that much, right, or they wouldn't have had me." It was about me, after all: I was the proof.

Jocelyn stared at me, longer than a pause, then brushed some hair out of Madison's eyes.

"Cameron! Kyle! Three minutes!" she called.

I kept looking at Jocelyn.

"What?" she said. "I'm not getting into this conversation without Mom here."

"What conversation?"

"You need to talk to Mom," she said.

"Talk about what?" It now seemed like my father must have known when he signed up that he'd get killed in Iraq, and he decided to do that rather than stick around to watch me grow up. Was it because I cried a lot as a baby? I couldn't help thinking if I'd been cuter, more complacent, he might not have gone.

"You know you're exactly like him," Jocelyn said, as

Kyle and Cameron charged into the room and dove toward their cereal bowls.

"Like who?" I said, willing her to mean our dad, Gary Hazenbrenner, but the more I wished, the more I understood. It was like washing pollen off your windshield, having that one clear area in the middle of everything made you realize how murky the rest of it was. Was it possible that I looked nothing like Dad because — and if he wasn't my dad, was it possible that —

"Who who?" Cameron asked.

"Who! Who!" said Kyle, imitating an owl. Madison tugged on Jocelyn's hair like she was riding a pony.

"Did they? Is that why . . ."

Cameron and Kyle gulped down their milk and ran to get their book bags. Jocelyn wriggled Madison into a sweater.

"Mom asked me once if I thought you knew, and I said no, I honestly don't think so, and she said, Cait, your sister Cait? She's the smartest person this family's ever had; if anyone could figure it out, she could. And I said maybe, but do you really want her to figure it out? You have to tell her. And she said yeah, but I knew she wouldn't. I don't know why all the work of this family falls on me."

I followed Jocelyn and her kids to the car.

"But why — "

"Who knows? They got married so young. I mean, I know I did too, but I'm just saying I can kind of see. And

Jekyllnheid, I mean Tom, Mom knew him from church, and he got her to go back to school. And I used to think he was okay, before. He has some good qualities when he's not drinking. I mean, when I said you guys were alike, I meant the good stuff."

"Good stuff?"

Jocelyn sighed. "Ask Mom."

■ ■ ■

My mom was home more because the college closed for a week after graduation every year, and the support staff had to take a week off without pay. One night, she was in the living room, soaking her feet and looking through four months of catalogs that had come in the mail. She liked spreading out her Christmas shopping so the bills didn't all come at once and so she could spend December making glittery cookies. She had a whole closet full of Christmas wrap she bought on sale every January.

"Mom?" I moved a pile of catalogs off a chair and sat down. Pittsburgh Pirates fans cheered from the TV in the bedroom where Tom was watching.

"Mmm?" My mom adjusted her glasses to read some fine print. A postcard asking, "Are your friends missing Country Style?" fluttered to the ground.

"Jocelyn and I were talking."

My mom put her catalog down on the stack on the

table. "This better not be about her stupid computer," she said. "If I hear one more word about that computer — "

"It's not," I said.

"Well, thank God."

"It's . . . she said some stuff — "

My mom looked at me, flipping the corner of a catalog with her thumb.

"I mean, was Dad, did you — when did you and Tom first get together?" I wished for a catalog I could ruffle, anything to keep from it being just me and Mom and the Truth.

"Look, I don't know what your sister told you — "

"She didn't tell me anything."

"I'm gonna kill that girl," my mom said. "Her and her theories. Tom's got theories too, and I guess I've got theories. Give us all a medal. But finding out for sure because of her stupid curiosity might take you from two daddies to zero."

I stared at her.

"You know, if it turned out your real daddy died in Iraq."

Another cheer from the baseball game on TV.

"But you can't — "

"Well, I expected you'd want to find out someday for sure. And when you're eighteen, you can put in the paperwork, require that DNA test or what have you. But I hope you'll remember — whatever turns out, I hope you'll remember all Tom did for you, all those years."

128

"All Tom did for me?" All Tom did *to* me was more like it, and my mom knew it. And if she meant financially, well, wasn't she working too? As far as I was concerned, it was her paycheck that paid for my clothes and my food and the portion of the roof that was over my room.

"All I'm saying is, don't disrespect the one that brought you up. Especially if he did it without even knowing if you was his."

I ran to the doorway of my room.

"Tom Gillienheid did not bring me up," I shouted, not caring if he heard me over the TV. "And there is no way on earth I'm 'his.'"

But my mom didn't answer. Eventually, I drove myself back to my sister's house, where everyone was already asleep.

■ ■ ■

In the 284 days before I would turn eighteen and find out about my dad, the rest of the county was focused on the fire: who Rob Sullivan was; if Jeremy Greene was or wasn't involved; and, like Jocelyn had said, what the county was coming to. Every week at least three or four letters in the *Register* thanked the firefighters, complained about declining community values, and asked whether people would have cared as much about a trailer fire in Mount Jenkins. Everyone wanted to say where they'd been when they first heard about the fire. Jocelyn was going nuts, afraid she'd get in trouble for being at the sheriff's office, and that her friend the drunk dispatcher would lose his job. For all her worrying, you'd think she set that house on fire.

So of course I had to think about that night constantly, only for me it was about more than just the fire. If I wasn't who I thought I was, who was I? Was I anybody? Jeremy Greene didn't think I was anybody when he came running into the sheriff's office that night. And what was his story, anyway? If he was involved in the fire, wasn't it weird that he came into the sheriff's office that same night, probably right after setting the fire, and started talking about his friend? It didn't make sense that a band nerd like Jeremy Greene would do something like that, especially all by himself, and if he did do something like that all by himself, that he'd fly babbling into the sheriff's office right after. Something besides the mess with my stepfather wasn't right.

■ ■ ■

I had to make sure Jeremy wouldn't say anything at the trial that would get my sister or that dispatcher in trouble. (That was the reason I wanted to talk to Jeremy. Wasn't it?) So in the fall of senior year, I started hanging around marching band practice after school, watching the band members parade around the football field and make formations. I kept watching, even after I realized Jeremy had been kicked out of band, because it seemed like some answer or another would emerge if only I studied the band's patterns closely enough. Either that, or the truth would come out and Jeremy would be back. Everyone would laugh about how they thought he had set fire to somebody's house, and life would go back to normal.

The bleachers were hard, and by the end of practice I was sitting on my hands to keep them warm. I never knew how much practice it took to have a marching band be one of the top four in the state for the last fifteen years. Their songs stuck in my head even more than Madison's, so I'd be sitting in class and suddenly hear "The Lion Sleeps Tonight." I had become a marching band groupie.

I might have kept watching the band forever, I guess, if it hadn't been for Paula Delacorte, this trombone player who was so big she had to special-order her clothes over the Internet.

"Why are you watching us practice all the time?" she said.

"No reason." I took out my history homework as if that was my plan all along, to sit on the bleachers and do homework to "Another One Bites the Dust." But it was too cold to hold my pen without keeping my hand in my sleeve.

"Nobody watches the marching band for no reason."

Paula narrowed her eyes, and I realized how stupid this was. I shoved my homework into my backpack and climbed down the bleachers.

I planned to shortcut through the building to get to the sheriff's office, where I could hang around until Jocelyn got off work. But I didn't get very far before I finally bumped into Jeremy in the lobby near the band room. Not the front lobby, where there was a big trophy showcase from when our school had a winning football team in the 1980s, but the dinky lobby near the band room, where my stupid essay about what I would do if I were governor had been hanging for almost a year. Jeremy was leaning against some lockers with his eyes closed. His open backpack was next to him, and I could see a mess of crumpled papers inside.

"Hi," I said.

He squinted up at me and closed his eyes again. "Hi."

"I know it's none of my business," I began.

"But you're gonna say it anyway."

"I just gotta know: did you really set that fire? You were saying all that about your friend — was it just a coincidence you left right when that stuff came in on the scanner?" I sounded like an idiot, like a teenager. I hated sounding like a teenager.

"You're right," Jeremy said. "It's none of your business." He put his backpack over both shoulders and

132

started walking toward the front of the school. I hurried after him.

"Could you please leave me alone?" he said.

"My sister could get in trouble," I said. "I have to know what's going on."

Someone was sitting on a bench outside the main office, near the elderly guppies who barely have strength to swim back and forth in their tank. When he stood up, I saw it was Jeremy's brother Albert, the one who was retarded or something.

Jeremy told me, "You can't know, okay? Maybe I don't even know."

"Hi, Jeremy!" Albert said too loudly. I had known him my whole life but couldn't remember ever hearing him talk.

"Hi, Albert," said Jeremy.

"Are you Jeremy's girlfriend?" Albert asked me.

"No!" Jeremy and I both said at the same time, and Albert laughed.

"Cait was just leaving," Jeremy said.

"Too bad," Albert said. "Bye, Cait!"

"Bye," I said. I turned around and walked back toward the music room, even though I'd have to leave the building a different way and have a longer walk to downtown. I could always tell Jocelyn I took longer because I was talking to boys; that would make her laugh.

■ ■ ■

"Maybe I don't even know," Jeremy had said. How can someone not know if they've burned a house down? But I know more than most people about not-knowing for as long as possible, about choosing to stay in a comfortable darkness you can never return to once you decide to Know. And about how not-knowing is a kind of knowing, too.

I walked downtown with my hands in my pockets and my braid tucked into the back of my jacket. I was too old to play detective, not sexy enough to be an international spy. I was just Cait Hazenbrenner — and that was who I planned to stay. No more changing my name.

The grass at the edge of the Jacobys' farm was getting taller, and I brushed a stick against it as I walked. Their cow mailbox was globbed over with tar but had all the parts intact.

All the kids my age are dying to get out of here. A few will succeed, and the rest will get so burdened down with responsibilities, like my sister, that they can't ever change anything. They won't run for office or found an organization or (should I say it?) write a book that would be read by people in other places, people who have never even heard of Tillmon County and don't quite believe that real people actually live here — they won't do any of those things, so nothing will ever change. And the same thing will happen to me: either

I'll get a scholarship and go to college, and before I can turn around I'll have a life somewhere else, like my oddball cousin Rebekah who somehow is off becoming a doctor in Pittsburgh. Or, more likely, I'll get a job to pay for college, and I'll take a few classes here and there, maybe even get my two-year degree in about a decade or so, but by then I'll have kids and have to work all kinds of overtime to pay for stuff they need. So if I'm going to do something that matters, something that makes people pay attention to Tillmon County and maybe even makes things better here, I have to do it now, before my life goes off track.

I looked up to where the first leaves were turning, and for the first time since I was little, I believed that their fiery show wasn't just about death. Some of those leaves, after they fell, would work their way deep into the soil and give life to something in the spring. I took out a pen and my history notebook, which was still mostly empty. I flipped the notebook upside-down so it was almost (but not quite) like starting at the beginning. What had been the last page was now the first page. I didn't know yet what I would say, but I was ready to write.

The Trial

Lacey

My family mostly stopped going to church after my brother died. But around the time my dad found out about his heart problem and I started thinking I just cannot go through this all over again, the Church of the Holy Redeemer out on Route 329 started having Sunday night teen fellowship meetings, and sometimes I would go. Which is relevant only because they don't care there what anybody wears, which is pretty refreshing for anywhere in this county, and it was how I found myself without anything appropriate to wear for the trial. Finally I borrowed a navy blue jacket from my mother, but it was tight under the arms and no matter how much I tugged on the sleeves, too much of my white blouse stuck out over each wrist.

My mom never talked to me directly about the miscarriage, but since then she had acted kind of hesitant, like patting my shoulder in a not-quite lead-in to a hug when she came to my room to bring me the jacket. Amelia says it's because my mom and I have both lost a child now, but I don't think that's it. Amelia doesn't always think very carefully about how her opinions are going to sound to other people.

I can't complain, though. When Amelia found out both my parents had to work the day of the trial, she insisted on being there for me and convinced her parents that it would be more educational in terms of learning about the American justice system than anything she'd miss in school that day, which was probably true, and anyway the kind of argument likely to work with parents who drive all the way to Pittsburgh to see a new exhibit at the art museum or hear an author they like at Barnes and Noble. Some people are just in denial that they live in the middle of nowhere, which I guess is one way to approach it. Anyway, they were so convinced by her argument that they took the day off work too — Amelia's dad teaches at the college and her mom works from home, editing educational software — and they sat right next to her, absorbing the beauty of the American justice system. Maybe it really is a beautiful system for people who don't count the DUI cases in the *Register* each week and wonder what's the point of a system that couldn't save Jacob. Or maybe Amelia's parents came because they found out about her plan to run away to California and they were afraid to let her stay home from school unsupervised.

Either way, the three of them sitting in the back of the courtroom made it easier to pretend I was just talking to them, answering the lawyer's questions about what Aiden and Jeremy and Albert bought that morning at the store.

"That's the only part they'll care about," Amelia had reminded me the night before, and as crazy as it seemed that a room full of people might care more about what brand lighter fluid Aiden bought than the loss of what would have become a human life — well, I've seen enough crazy things that I guess this one should not have surprised me.

amelia

so it was a way to get out of school, plus be there for lacey, because maybe i still felt a little guilty about ignoring her phone calls the day she lost her baby and sold lighter fluid to the guys who burned down that house by the lake. plus i was bored out of my mind, because even though i was technically un-grounded from charging the plane ticket, my parents were still watching my every move. but they bought my whole speech about learning about our justice system from watching lacey testify. i think that california thing finally got it through their heads that i'm never going to be a brainiac like they are or like they thought they were signing up for when they adopted a six-month-old baby from china.

but here's the crazy part. i spent most of the trial watching the lawyer for the county, who, to be honest, did not look like much of a brainiac. she looked like she could use a better haircut and someone to give her a couple of magazines from this decade with some advice about what outfits she should not even think about wearing, but mostly what i noticed was this look that i recognized immediately because i've felt the same way every single day of my life. it was in the way she walked across the courtroom, one foot in front of the other, like she had more important things to care about than what any of us thought of her shoes. it was in her face when she asked questions to the witnesses and when she returned to her seat and ruffled through her papers with unmanicured fingernails. the look said, *"it's not fair."*

if anyone understood *not fair,* it was me. lately i'd been lying awake thinking about what lacey had asked me after ben and i broke up. "do you think ben could be gay?" she'd said, finally putting words to the off-balance feeling i'd had for months and especially since that afternoon of the gerbera daisies, when it felt like ben went through the motions step-by-step, like sex was no different from building a birdhouse, no emotion required.

this lawyer, i could tell, understood how truly *not fair* it was, but instead of making idiotic plans to move to california, or driving herself crazy about whether life would be more fair or less fair if her ex-boyfriend turned out to be gay, this woman was trying to make one little piece of the world a little bit more fair for someone else.

i could do that too, although with a better haircut and shoes. becoming a lawyer would mean about another hundred years in school, so i'd have to decide if it was worth sitting in a classroom all those extra years, plus giving my parents the satisfaction of being right, but it was something to think about.

lacey, of course, did great at the trial, and afterwards my parents bought both of us lunch at the big spruce creamery.

Ben

When I drove out to the falls that Saturday night, I didn't even know about the fire. No one did yet, I guess. I just needed a place to hide in the car all night and maybe pretend to sleep, which seemed easier than explaining why I wasn't camping overnight with the hiking club. If I couldn't have Rob's arms around me, at least I could have the rushing water drown out my thoughts. It was the best escape I knew of, and it was legal and free. The fact that Rob might be there too hadn't even occurred to me, at least not consciously, but the way he sped away as soon as I arrived made me realize what I had done.

I spent most of Sunday composing an apology note, revising it over and over until I couldn't stand it anymore, then crumpling it up, only to start all over again five minutes later. Finally, just before bed, I wrote in the middle of a sheet of paper, "We need to talk," and I drew a couple of scenes from the falls in case they might make my case for me. I folded the paper carefully and put it in my physics notebook to give to him during lab.

Although why I thought Rob would be in physics on Monday, and where in this county I thought he might have slept after his house burned down, I have no idea. It was pure idiocy to think Rob would be in school Monday, especially with everyone talking all day like the fire (and in fact Rob Sullivan himself) had happened for their personal amusement, to make up for some of the monotony of living in Tillmon County. But I still don't think it was stupid to assume he'd be back eventually. Not that he owed me a goodbye or anything, but I refused to believe that someone else I cared about would disappear completely from my life. Still, all of the lengthy email explanations and chatty, not-trying-too-hard text messages I composed over the next few weeks sounded so stupid that I deleted them without hitting send.

If I could have just seen him in person, I was sure I could have found the right thing to say, or I could have taken him to some new spot at the falls where we could have sat together and let the water say everything. But when that wasn't possible, I did the only logical thing in my increasingly illogical world: I broke up with Amelia. She kept flipping her hair the whole time I bumbled through my explanation about how we only had one more year of high school and we both should get to know some other people before we were supposed to decide on things for the rest of our lives or whatever. I didn't mention that I guessed the rest of my life had already been more or less decided without me. Amelia just nodded, which caused her finger to get tangled in the hair she was flipping, and she said she had been thinking the same thing. I was almost glad for the

142

hair-flipping and hoped I had left her unharmed enough to find some guy who would find that charming or sexy, or at least less annoying than I did.

When my mom asked, I told her it was by mutual decision, which offered the unexpected benefit that my mom assumed Amelia broke up with me, and so I didn't have to offer any explanation for why I was moping around the house. On Sunday afternoons, I drove out to Ruggers Mountain, about twenty miles in the opposite direction from Yellowbelly Falls, and found a spot high up where I could pick up NPR. So as far as my mom knew, the hiking club kept meeting all the way until the end of the school year.

To be fair, my mom could be forgiven for not keeping up with every detail of the hiking club's activities. Because one afternoon when she had gone to take a bag of just-picked lettuce from our garden over to Aunt Phyllis, the doorbell rang, and Lenny, our mailman, was standing there with a registered letter. And even though I knew it was the wrong thing to do, I told myself that opening it was the only way to know if I should call my aunt's house or even drive out there myself.

Part of me had been waiting for this registered letter for five years, since the day my father left on his scavenger hunt for God. At first, the un-finalized divorce seemed to leave open a window for my father's return, but after a while I figured maybe my father thought it wasn't worth the bother, that the whole fact of their marriage, not to mention my sisters and me, were too much for him to acknowledge.

So the document itself, and the gist of what it was saying didn't come as a surprise, but the name at the top sent a jolt down my spine. I read that first paragraph three or four times: "This Property Settlement Agreement, which will be referred to as the 'Agreement,' is made by Nadav Krupin (formerly Nicholas Wayne Krupin) and Linda Krupin," etc., etc. And finally it hit me like I imagine Lot's wife must have felt when one minute she's walking around like a regular person, and the next minute she's frozen into a pillar of something she must know will dissolve with the first sprinkle of rain. Of course all the Google searches in the world hadn't led me to my father, because my father, Nick Krupin, no longer existed.

That night I found him on the second page of Google results, Nadav Krupin at an accounting firm in Brooklyn, New York. I found email addresses and phone numbers, and even photos of all the senior-level accountants, in case any doubt remained about whether Nadav and Nick could really be the same person.

At one a.m. I decided: if he had to have a new name, I was glad it was something crazy-sounding like "Nadav," because if his only purpose was to hide from me, "John" or "Bill" would have worked just fine. He must have had some other reason. And I realized that as strange as "Nadav" sounded to my Tillmon County ears, Nick — and especially that "Wayne" — would have sounded just as strange in his new life among Orthodox Jews in Brooklyn, New York. Maybe worse than strange, if he tried to make himself over as an observant Jew and all anyone could think of was St. Nicholas.

At two a.m. I started thinking about the New York address — okay, it was in Brooklyn, but how far could that be from the New York people talked about, the one where Rob was from? The fact that Rob Sullivan and Nadav Krupin were living

144

anywhere near each other — was it a grand cosmic coincidence, or was New York so big that it was like being amazed to find the two people you missed most were both in the Western Hemisphere?

I poked around the site for a while, reading where the different accountants went to college and things. It was after two-thirty, and I had my physics final the next day, including a lab portion that I had opted to do myself rather than join an existing pair. I couldn't email Nadav Krupin, because an email sent at this hour would look like I had been lying awake thinking of him, and make him imagine I'd been doing that since the day he left. But I could check out Greyhound schedules, imagining routes where I could either drive to Carter Springs and change buses in Washington, D.C., or else drive to Pittsburgh and get a direct bus. And I could MapQuest his office in relation to the Greyhound terminal in New York.

■ ■ ■

As the trial got closer, the fire gossip started up again — about who did it, of course, but also about whether Rob and his family had any right to be in our county in the first place. This is what happens when houses get too fancy, people seemed to say, as if the house itself, with all the fancy designer clothes, had spontaneously combusted.

But I was less focused on this than I might have been, because by then I had emailed the man I used to think of as my father. When he didn't write back for a week, I almost gave up, but it turned out he was on vacation, and we exchanged three or four emails during the summer. Nothing dramatic or whatever, and at times it was hard thinking of things to write about that didn't get too close to anything that was actually important in my life. Toward the end of August, he finally invited me for a visit, maybe figuring by then I'd say I was too busy with school starting. But we found a weekend in mid-October, and my mom said I could miss school on a Friday so I could get to New York before the Jewish Sabbath. Later I'd wonder why she was OK with me going off to visit my crazy semi-father. Maybe she had decided he had no more power over us now that the divorce was almost final, or maybe, now that I was almost eighteen, she realized that if I was going to change my religion or otherwise jump off the deep end, keeping me off the Greyhound bus was not the solution. Anyway, I convinced her somehow and bought my ticket. I had no idea that it would be the same day as the trial.

■ ■ ■

Now, standing in the back of the courtroom, I don't even know if Rob can see me. I search for some kind of sign I can flash, some way I can let Rob know I'm here for him by touching my ear or scratching my eyebrow. But we never worked out any secret sign, maybe because we never knew each other that well after all, or maybe because our life is not a spy movie. I leave right after Rob's testimony. I have a long drive, and a bus to catch.

Rob

It's hard to lose faith in humanity
when the people you live with grow heirloom tomatoes
and two kinds of garlic, and also kale,
which sounds like it would make me gag
but is actually pretty good when my aunt's partner, Tamara,
brushes it with olive oil and sea salt
and bakes the leaves until they're crispy.
They also make their own pizza
every Friday night,
with organic whole wheat flour,
and we eat it on beautiful plates they rescue from flea markets
and watch foreign movies on their flat-screen TV
while Aunt Lucy rubs Tamara's feet.

So I have been eating healthier,
and this summer I did a drama thing
at Carnegie Mellon,
where the director said I had potential
and that he'd love to hear from me next year
if I get my SAT scores up.
So I've been studying more, too,
of all things.

My parents sent money
and I got a new suit at Nordstrom's,
which they do have in Pittsburgh, surprisingly.
And I think, too bad for you, Ben Krupin.
You weren't ready for me.
But who can blame you, with me looking so good,
as I straighten my collar and decide
how many earrings to wear for the trial.
(Aunt Lucy and I compromise
on one.)

I could have mentioned
to a lot of people
that someone was supposed to be
with me
that night:
my parents, my aunts, my therapist,
my new friends who actually know both places I've lived
and stay friends with me anyway.
At first my version of the story skipped over Ben,
because what kind of loser gets stood up
by his boyfriend of three months?
But after a while I skipped over him
because even if Ben waited
a hundred more years to come out,

I'd keep his secret that long.
It's the least I can do for the guy who saved my life,
even by accident.

I was only on the witness stand a minute,
but that was long enough for everyone
to admire my suit
and wonder what made my skin look so good.
(I know they didn't guess kale.)
Ben was there;
he'd put on weight.
My friend Cynthia would have asked what I'd seen in him,
but not in a mean way.
Afterwards, Tamara suggested lunch
at the Big Spruce or else
one of the fancy places by the lake
that were always empty
when my parents and I used to get take-out.
I was starving, but I said
let's get on the road.

Cait

I skip school for the first time in my life to watch a trial that, technically, has nothing to do with me. I am even more invisible than usual, which is saying a lot.

Watching Aiden on the witness stand, I thought about how he looked as a first-grader in his too-small T-shirts, and I remembered how my misfit cousin Rebekah had babysat him for a little while around that time. Geeky, loner Rebekah, the one who finished medical school and stayed in Pittsburgh for her residency, even though I have to say that Rebekah, no offense intended, is about the last person I'd want poking around my body.

Whatever, she had made it out, so maybe she wasn't as weird as I had always thought. When the trial ended, I decided, I'd call Aunt Helaine for Rebekah's address so I could send her the news article about her former babysitting charge. Rebekah wouldn't write back, of course, but I'd think about that little piece of the *Register* breaking free and flying out into the world, and I'd think about the day when my story would, too.

Albert

Sometimes, after Jeremy goes to sleep, I lie awake for a long time and watch his blanket move up and down while he breathes. Only sometimes it stops moving, and I know he is awake, worrying about what happened. It's hard to know how much I helped him that night in the woods and how much, as usual, I messed things up worse. With bottlecaps, you can say for sure that this one completes a set and this other one is all wrong. People are trickier. So this morning before the trial, I asked Jeremy, "Are you sure you want me there?" And he said, "You're on the witness list — you've gotta come." I thought about the people in Tennessee, Ohio, and Saskatchewan who I met on the Internet and who count on trading with me for authentic bottlecaps they can't get where they live. And now a whole courtroom full of people was counting on me, too. Whether or not I had helped Jeremy before, I was helping him today. I puffed out about three shirt sizes just thinking about that.

Jeremy

When the school found out about my involvement with the fire, I was no longer allowed to participate in extracurriculars, which included marching band.

"I'm very disappointed, Jeremy," the band teacher, Mr. Macomb, told me when I turned in my uniform, crumpled into a Food Fair bag. At first I didn't know if he meant the fire or my treatment of the uniform. Then he said, "We were counting on you for Battle of the Bands," and I realized his disappointment didn't have much to do with me at all.

Kids at school avoided me, with one exception. In the halls, at my locker, in the cafeteria, I kept seeing that girl Cait from the sheriff's office. At first I thought maybe I just hadn't noticed her before, like when I learn a new piece on the trumpet,

I hear phrases from it everywhere, in the phone buttons or in change dropping on the floor.

Then she talked to me. Finally, one afternoon this fall Cait started asking about the fire. I tried to read her face, to see what she already knew, but I got distracted by her freckles.

So I was ruder than I meant to be. Because of those freckles, which were more beautiful than I thought freckles had a right to be. I said it was none of her business, and even though I regretted it right away, I didn't know how to take it back. But then she kept asking me if I really started the fire, and finally I said, "I don't know," to make her stop.

■ ■ ■

I dreamed that Cait visited me in the juvenile detention facility and we took a walk on a cobblestone path. I saw a movie once with a psychiatric hospital like that, but probably a juvenile facility around here wouldn't keep its bushes trimmed so nice. I dreamed Cait wrote me letters on thin, flower-scented stationery, with an old-fashioned pen.

"Why did you do it?" she'd write, and she wouldn't do anything stupid like put a smiley-face over the "i."

■ ■ ■

Before the trial, I practiced my answers in front of a mirror, trying both a "yes" and a "yes, sir," not knowing that the lawyer for the county would turn out to be a woman. Maybe that was what froze me up. Because when the woman lawyer asked, "Did you act alone?" I didn't answer.

My neck itched, but years of marching band taught me that you don't reach around to scratch.

They knew Aiden had been there that night, but they thought he was just along for the ride. What mattered was that I was the one to make the plan, to carry it out alone.

"Did you act alone?" the woman lawyer repeated. Her navy blue suit was wrinkled in the back, and she swung her arms when she walked.

I cleared my throat. Cait wouldn't write me letters. And while I washed dishes or dug holes or whatever people in juvie did all day, Aiden would set more fires. How had I gotten here, from letting him copy my answers on a vocabulary pre-assessment to covering for him while he set people's houses (because how could he stop at just one house) on fire? It was right that Lindsey won that award at music camp last summer: I didn't deserve to be Most Valuable Brass Player, or Most Valuable Anything.

The woman lawyer said, "Mr. Greene, you are required to answer: did you act alone?"

I inhaled, wheezing slightly.

"No, ma'am," I said. And time stopped.

After that, it was like people were shouting into the wrong end of a megaphone: I could hear the words but had to work hard to understand what anything meant. I wondered if every day was like that for Albert.

I told them about Aiden's plan, making sure to mention how he wanted to get not just himself but the whole county ready for Jesus, so at least people would know he had a good purpose in mind.

"Who lit the match?" the lawyer asked, and I said: "We both did."

"How could two people light the same match?"

So I had to explain how, with all Aiden's planning and all our careful preparations, when it came down to that moment, our only matches were under the floor mat of my dad's truck, where some orange soda had spilled a few months earlier. So we each tried a few times, with a few matches, and when we thought we heard something behind us, we looked at each other and ran, not knowing there was a fire.

I didn't add that even today, I was certain there was no fire when we left.

■ ■ ■

Lacey Miller had circles under her eyes and kept tugging at the ends of her sleeves while she testified. I saw Albert watch her wrists disappear into the sleeves and reappear again, and saw Albert's breath rise up and down, his fingers tap together. Our parents were on each side of him, my dad in a suit and a Dollar General necktie. Mr. Jacoby was behind them, and when he testified, he talked about fixing Elsie as "doing repairs on my letterbox." Cait was in the back of the room by herself, but when I tried to catch her eye, she looked away.

Aiden's lawyer was a skinny guy who looked like he'd rather be selling tobacco and candy bars at the Quik-Mart. He asked Lacey what we bought at the hardware store, and if she noticed us doing anything unusual. She didn't.

Then the lawyer asked, "Was anyone else with them?"

"Yes, Jeremy's brother," she said. I glanced at Albert. This was the longest he had ever been allowed to stare at Lacey Miller.

"Mm-hmm!" the lawyer said. "And did Albert Greene say or do anything to make you think he was part of the plans to set the fire?"

"No, ma'am," Lacey answered quickly. "I don't think he'd be capable of it."

"Tell us what you mean."

"He's got too big a heart," Lacey said. "I've gone to school with him my whole life, and I've never seen him do an unkind thing to anybody."

"Objection, speculation," the woman lawyer said, and the judge said, "Sustained." But Albert was grinning like Lacey had said she'd marry him.

■ ■ ■

The lawyer asked Aiden: "Who accompanied you to Miller's Hardware the morning of April 22?"

Aiden said, "You know that already. Jeremy and his brother."

"And for the record, when you say, 'his brother,' you're referring to Albert Greene?"

"He's only got one brother."

"And did Albert Greene have any further role in the events of April 22?"

Aiden paused.

Just a short pause, and how could anyone know what someone meant by a pause? But I saw him glance at Albert (who, thank God, still had that ridiculous grin on his face, a grin that must have reminded the lawyers he didn't tie his shoes until fifth grade and made them decide against calling him to the witness stand). I imagined that Aiden had figured it out, that he knew that I would do for Albert what I would never in a million years do for him.

Aiden said, "I don't involve retards in my plans."

It was the first time I hadn't wanted to beat up whoever called my brother a retard. I was so focused on that word that it took me a minute to realize Aiden had also used a more important word. "My."

■ ■ ■

Did I act alone? Since the trial, Albert falls asleep every night smiling. When I lie in bed, watching his relaxed breathing, I hear the lawyer asking over and over: *Did you act alone?* And I still don't know.

Rob Sullivan shouldn't have had to lose his house, even if it was a nicer house than ninety-nine percent of the world would ever get to even look at. It's not his fault he's rich, and I don't think it's even his fault he likes other guys. I know what we did was wrong, but that's not quite the same as being sorry. "Sorry" would mean I'm not somehow better off than I was before, that I didn't accomplish my goal for junior year of doing something that mattered. Even if what mattered turned out to be saving Albert.

In the end I got two thousand hours of community service. I can do a lot of them over the summer and at the sheriff's office Christmas drive. At the Christmas drive, the regular volunteers work side-by-side with the "volunteers" working off mandatory hours, so you can't tell who's who. Back in ninth grade, while I was sorting macaroni and cheese boxes, someone had asked me what I was in for. I had liked thinking I looked tough enough for mandatory community service.

Maybe I'll ask Cait if she wants to volunteer with me. She wouldn't mind me asking, anyway, wouldn't laugh at me for suggesting it. I still don't know if my dream girl exists, someone who won't mind me and Albert someday living next door to each other and Albert coming over every night to eat supper and work on his bottlecap collection. But if a girl like that does exist, I bet she's something like Cait.

■ ■ ■

Some people want to set fires, I guess, and a few people even want their houses burned down, want to have people shake their heads and say how bad they have it. But for most of us, I think, our biggest fear is passing through life unnoticed, that when we die, we'll be another anonymous nobody from a place nobody heard of.

Did I act alone? I'm a twin; I've never acted alone in my life. Even when I practice my trumpet at home, I can hear the rest of the band around me.

Does anyone act alone? Maybe some places, where everyone doesn't know each other and a person can sneeze without the whole county knowing about it — maybe in those places, people act alone. But in Tillmon County, I don't think it's possible to act alone even if you want to.

Anyway, most of us, I think, don't want to act alone. We want to be part of the band.

Postscript

The Babysitter

When Aiden McNalley started first grade at South Branch Elementary, he wore rolled-up jeans and a T-shirt that said "Atlanta Braves" because that was where his father lived that year. Usually his arms were crossed in front of his chest so only the bottom of the Braves' emblem tomahawk was visible. In a red insulated lunch bag he carried his peanut butter sandwich (sliced diagonally), one green apple, four chocolate chip cookies, and a juice box.

The day Aiden started first grade, his mother began her new job as a receptionist for the Tillmon County Dental Clinic. She packed her lunch (a fat-free strawberry yogurt cup and a packet of sunflower seeds) in a brown plastic bag from Food Fair, although she would later realize she had forgotten a spoon, so she would anxiously eat a few bites by scooping the yogurt with the lid but end up throwing most of it away, telling herself she wasn't hungry. She was twenty-five and slept with the previous year's Tillmon Community College course schedule on her nightstand.

She would carpool each morning with a neighbor who worked as an X-ray technician at the hospital, next door to the dental clinic. She could wait with Aiden at his bus stop in the morning and be dropped off at home an hour after his afternoon bus rumbled down Second Street.

So for one hour each day, Aiden would be babysat by a serious girl named Rebekah who wore big plastic-framed glasses and had taken a babysitting course at Tillmon Community Action. Her mother ran a day care center in their home, and Rebekah's dream was to do the same thing, but the year after she babysat Aiden, her tenth-grade biology teacher would notice her aptitude for science, and two years later that teacher would help her win a scholarship to Flanders State. Four years after that, the same high school teacher would help Rebekah with her applications for medical school, and when it came time to choose her residency, Rebekah would surprise everyone by saying she wanted nothing whatsoever to do with children. One day she would win an award from the Gerontological Society of America for her research using birds to simulate the aging of the human brain.

When Rebekah babysat, she brought a green canvas tote bag filled with books, Popsicle sticks, crayons, and a few other things from Dollar General to make her "the most dynamic babysitter south of the lake," as she claimed on her flyers. She posted flyers wherever people let her: the library; the Glo, Baby, Glo! laundromat; Food Fair; Head Start. It was hard to say which of Rebekah's flyers Aiden's mother responded to. She had likely seen so many that by the time she noticed one, she felt like the most dynamic babysitter south of the lake was already an old friend.

When Rebekah brought the green tote bag to school, it attracted attention from the popular girls in her class. "Great Green Monster," they called her, and "Babyzilla." But she didn't care, or pretended not to, which was almost the same.

■ ■ ■

Afterward, she wondered: if she had acted like she cared about the names, would that have stopped them from going further? And when she read about Aiden in the newspaper, she wondered again: if she had stopped things from going further that day in the woods, could she somehow have prevented that fire?

■ ■ ■

At Rebekah's apartment near the University of Pittsburgh Medical Center, she sometimes went five, six days without checking her mail. Even when she brought the mail upstairs, the catalogs and credit card offers piled up on her coffee table, then under the coffee table, until some night when she couldn't study another minute and was about to say to hell with her whole medical career (approximately once every two months), she would cram the whole pile into grocery sacks, stuff them into a shopping cart, and wheel them to the recycling bins behind her building. The dumpsters were scary in the middle of the night, and each trip there Rebekah swore was her last one, but soon she would decide to go forward with medicine after all, the next day's mail would arrive, and the piles would begin again.

That was how Rebekah learned what happened with Aiden, three weeks after it appeared in the paper. She was in the elevator of her apartment building with the recycling sack sometime after midnight, when a hand-written envelope from her cousin Cait (a spelling change she heartily approved of) caught her attention. She had no idea how old Cait was by then, or what might have compelled her to write, but she opened the envelope there in the elevator, and Aiden McNalley's picture practically leapt out at her, he looked that similar to the six-year-old boy she remembered. When she got to the first floor, Rebekah sat down near the back entrance to her building, the one that the receptionist sometimes propped open for a friend who stole electronics from careless graduate students (although that wouldn't be discovered for several months). Rebekah sat by the door and read, and afterward she stared at her reflection in the dirty glass door pane until the sky lightened and her image blended into the recycling bins outside, like a hologram. Then she folded the article into a tiny square and threw out the rest of her mail.

■ ■ ■

The year Rebekah was "the most dynamic babysitter south of the lake," Aiden the first-grader lived only a mile from the high school, but it was closer to three miles by the time you cut around Muddy Falls. Rebekah didn't mind; she liked watching the leaves fall from the trees, the icicles form, and new leaves come out in the spring. It was a way of counting down how many years she had left until graduation. Adulthood was her only hope. When she walked to Aiden's house, the girls who tormented her — Misty and Ashlee and Jemma were their names — would call to her and try to trip her and follow her to Second Street, where they would turn left to head into town, and Rebekah would go straight, until the street ended.

Rebekah imagined how they must have decided to follow her to Aiden's house. It was still winter-coat weather, but by afternoon the coats were blowing open, hats and scarves left behind at school. One of the girls — Misty, most likely, who wore her hair in a tight ponytail — probably dared the other two to follow Rebekah, and the others probably laughed, until one of them (Jemma, maybe, whose father was a county commissioner) said, "I'll do it if you do it." Three years later, just before graduation, Jemma's father would be convicted of accepting bribes. He would lose his job at Owenbraun's Chevrolet and serve six months at the Tillmon County Detention Center, while Jemma's mother went to work selling pocketbooks at the Bon-Ton in Carter Springs.

Misty, Ashlee, and Jemma didn't make any secret of following Rebekah, giggling and shrieking like they were choosing outfits for Homecoming. So let them follow me, Rebekah thought. It's a free country.

"Stop it!" Rebekah heard them squeal, and "I can't help it!" and "Hey, wait up!" Their voices were so shrill that it was impossible to feel afraid. They weren't used to hiking in mud or getting their clothes dirty. Probably they would get bored and go home, but if they didn't, so what? The babysitting course covered fires and choking and poisonous substances, but Rebekah could not recall any mention of renegade fourteen-year-old girls.

On the other side of Muddy Falls, Rebekah exited the park and walked half a mile down Second Street, where she waited for Aiden's bus and where Misty, Ashlee, and Jemma ducked furtively into the Quik-Mart. Later, Rebekah would notice powdery sugar from Quik-Mart doughnuts on her coat, Aiden's coat, Aiden's backpack. She wondered if you could catch a fingerprint in dough-nut sugar, but the sugar fell away wherever she touched it.

Aiden was always last off the bus, trudging off as if he'd spent the day in the mines, not in first grade with Mrs. Clotfelter, who Rebekah happened to know was an excellent teacher. Rebekah remembered feeling proud to be in that class, to be in the Blue Jays reading group and finally have homework to spread out on the dining room table. But if Mrs. Clotfelter was still assigning homework, you wouldn't know it from Aiden.

Aiden never said much as he and Rebekah walked to his house, which was a townhouse specially built for people with Section 8 housing vouchers. That meant fresh paint and sunlight, and cheap carpet that came untacked and closet doors that slid off their tracks. Once, Rebekah brought a *Superfudge* poster she got free at the library and helped Aiden tack it up in his room, but it was gone the next day. When she asked about it, Aiden's mother said she had taken it down to frame it, but it never reappeared and Rebekah didn't ask again.

Lately, Aiden had started walking several paces behind Rebekah, the way Rebekah had walked behind her parents when they were in public and she didn't want anyone to know that the bearded man with the bowtie and the woman with the homemade dress were her parents. They were walking down the street this way, Rebekah carrying Aiden's backpack and red lunch bag, when Rebekah heard a small shriek, like a smoke detector announcing its batteries needed to be changed. When Rebekah turned, Aiden was surrounded by Misty, Ashlee, and Jemma.

"Hey," she shouted. "Leave him alone!" But none of the girls looked up.

"You're a cutie pie," Misty was telling Aiden. She put her finger under his chin as if to tickle him, but Aiden batted it away. His elbows, his haircut, even his eyebrows were sharp and angular.

"You don't like to be tickled?" Jemma asked. "I thought all little boys liked being tickled."

Aiden turned to run, but he plowed straight into Ashlee's legs, and she caught him firmly by the shoulders.

"Hey!" Rebekah said again, prying Ashlee's fingers loose. "Let go of him!"

Ashlee giggled harder, and Aiden, momentarily free, raced past Rebekah and back toward the woods.

"Get back here!" Rebekah yelled, chasing him. She turned and called over her shoulder to Misty, Ashlee, and Jemma. "Idiots!"

They laughed. Rebekah roamed around for several minutes listening to Aiden and the girls get closer and then further away, then closer again. She hadn't lasted long in the Girl Scouts, where she imagined she would have learned about navigating in the woods, or some other skill that would have helped her in this situation. Or maybe that was only the Boy Scouts.

■ ■ ■

When the whimpers and giggles stabilized to one location, Rebekah found the group in a clearing near the park entrance. Aiden was at the bottom of a heap, with Misty, Ashlee, and Jemma piled on top. His body was still, like someone who had grown too tired to protest.

"The tickle monster's coming!" Ashlee screamed, running her fingers all over Aiden's ribs.

"Laugh, dammit!" Misty shrieked.

Ashlee lifted Aiden's skinny arms and began tickling his armpits. Aiden was not wearing a coat, and his sweatshirt was balled up in the bag Rebekah was carrying.

"Tickle harder!" Misty demanded. She leaned against the Port-a-Potty that no one dared venture into during swimming season.

"Get away from him!" Rebekah barged past the shed and attempted to pull Ashlee and Jemma away.

"Ooh, it's the *babysitter*," said Misty.

"Look, she's making him cry," Jemma said. Sure enough, Aiden had lost his stoic expression and had returned to being a six-year-old boy.

"Aww, why does your babysitter make you cry?"

"Maybe you should find a new one."

Aiden sobbed harder as the tickling continued, but no tears came. He was like a stiff washcloth from which no more moisture could be squeezed.

"Leave him alone!" Rebekah shouted. And then, "Hey, somebody! Help!"

"Shut her up," Misty instructed. And before Rebekah knew what was happening, they had pulled off Aiden's striped T-shirt and stuffed it in her mouth.

"Give that back," Aiden said, surprised and sounding older. His eyes went from one girl to another.

"The tickle monster hasn't eaten yet today!" Ashlee shouted, running her fingers over Aiden's chest. His chest, between his ribs, was marked with scratches and bug bites. "The tickle monster gets hungry!"

Misty and Jemma sat on Rebekah's legs, and Misty tied Rebekah's hands together with Aiden's sweatshirt, which she must have gotten from the bag. The ground was cold and covered with dried leaves and twigs.

"Stop!" Aiden said again.

Misty continued to sit on Rebekah while Ashlee and Jemma tickled Aiden all over. They left his pants on, though at one point Ashlee reached a hand inside the waist of his little-boy jeans, stopping when she realized that the elastic of his underwear was threatening to tear. Aiden kicked at first and tried to shake them off, but finally lay limp on the ground, as if the tickling were happening to his body but his spirit were far away.

Rebekah didn't know how much time went by before the Dodge Ram pulled into the parking lot. Its silver paint twinkled with the promise of an older boy whose part-time job paid more than babysitting.

The truck slowed down as it approached.

"Hey," called the driver, a senior named Garrett. He was a friend of Ashlee's older brother, and he had a friend with him whose name none of them knew.

Ashlee stood up and fluffed her hair with her fingers.

"Hey," she said.

"Whatcha doing?"

"Nothing." Ashlee smiled her prettiest smile and touched a finger to the corner of her mouth, as if trying to remember whether she had reapplied lip gloss after P.E.

Misty and Jemma stood up too, and Rebekah stretched her legs gingerly, trying to see if anything was broken. Jemma leaned awkwardly to one side, as if to hide the half-naked boy and his bound-and-gagged babysitter. But Garrett didn't seem to notice anything unusual.

"Want to come to Sunny's?" he asked. Sunny's pizza was pathetic, everyone knew; they made their money from their video arcade and the fact that they would sell cigarettes without asking for ID. There were few places

Rebekah wanted to go less than she wanted to go to Sunny's.

"Okay," Ashlee said. She glanced at her friends, and Garrett seemed to remember them suddenly. Nobody remembered Rebekah or, especially, Aiden.

"Yeah, sorry we only have room for one," Garrett said. "But maybe we'll see you over there."

"Yeah, maybe," said Misty, as if fifteen miles were no big deal to a ninth-grader with no car.

Ashlee disappeared into the truck with a guilty wave to her friends, and Misty and Jemma stood around like girls at a dance, looking purposeful.

Finally, Misty said, "Ashlee slept over at my house one time and wet the bed."

"For real?"

Misty nodded. "My mom had to wash her sleeping bag and everything."

"Gross."

After a pause, Misty said, "These are totally not the right shoes for walking home."

"Do you think he'll be okay?" Jemma asked, nodding toward Aiden.

"I guess."

They turned and walked in the direction they had come from. Aiden waited a few minutes, then stood up and helped Rebekah untie the sweatshirt from around her hands. It was his sweatshirt, after all, and he wanted it back. He didn't know yet how stretched out it had gotten, how it would never fit the same.

■ ■ ■

Rebekah knew, of course, that none of this was Aiden's fault. But whenever she looked at him — she couldn't help it — she pictured him with his shirt off, the two of them held hostage by a gaggle of ridiculous adolescents with the combined IQ of a tree frog. To get angry at the girls would have meant admitting what had happened, what she had let happen. So instead of telling the girls what she thought of them, she began telling Aiden:

"Stop walking so slow."

"Make up your mind."

"Don't be stupid."

Instead of enjoying their hours together after school, she found herself calculating her rate of pay down to tiny fractions of an hour: ten minutes of giving Aiden a snack equaled one-sixth of her hourly rate. In this way the hours and days passed more bearably. Every other week, Rebekah took her earnings to the bank and made a deposit in her college account.

■ ■ ■

When Tillmon Health Services (which included the dental health clinic) began offering after-school child care, and a bus that would take Aiden directly from school to the clinic, Rebekah's babysitting days came to an end. Her dream of owning a day care center was replaced by so many better dreams that it hardly seemed a loss. But once in a while, she would notice someone being attacked: the dog in college who lived in a fraternity house and was forced to drink alcohol until he threw up; the chair of the social studies department at her high school, who was the subject of so many rumors that he finally resigned and took a lower-paying job in Flanders. Whenever Rebekah witnessed incidents like these, she was temporarily unable to breathe, as if something were stuffed in her mouth, and her instinct was to run, as if the attackers would come for her next.

It is thought that people who choose medical careers do so from a desire to help, to save others from disease and injury, but sometimes the opposite is true: sometimes they choose those careers because the long hours of training, the sleepless nights in understaffed, fluorescent-lit hospitals, the lifetime commitment to be on call for strangers provide a safe hiding place. Rebekah wouldn't have stated it that way, but she wouldn't have denied that living without sleep also meant living without worry, doubt, regret, and a thousand other things that people with regular jobs and regular lives had to face every day.

When she folded the picture of Aiden and put it in her wallet, she didn't expect to look at it much. If asked, she would have predicted it would stay there until the crease was so deep it blocked most of Aiden's face, and it might tumble out while she was searching for her ATM card, or else get thrown away with receipts when she got fed up at being unable to close her wallet. But she looked at the picture more than she would have guessed, even reaching into her wallet sometimes to feel the smooth newsprint without needing to take out the article.

When Rebekah moved back to Tillmon County to care for her mother, she bought an immaculate Victorian in downtown Spruce Valley for a third of what it would have cost in Pittsburgh and set up her practice on the ground level. Because she paid a high school girl (a homely girl who wasn't as bright as she first seemed and whose parents couldn't afford to pay for orthodontia) to bring her groceries, she seldom ran into her old classmates, but she was no longer afraid when she did. And after her mother died, when Rebekah realized she would stay in Tillmon County forever, she removed the creased photocopied article from her wallet and placed it in the top left drawer of her desk, where she saw it once a month when she paid her bills.

"Spruce Valley Man and Youth Convicted in April Arson," the headline said. Every time Rebekah saw "April Arson" capitalized like that, she thought it looked like a name, a girl detective who drove a jalopy around Tillmon County, looking for mysteries. It was a long article even for the *Tillmon Register*, which once devoted half a page to the retirement of South Branch Elementary's oldest employee, an 81-year-old cafeteria worker.

The article described how Aiden and a friend (unnamed, because the friend was a minor) set fire to one of the mini-mansions near the lake. The friend got community service, but Aiden got eight years in jail.

"Crazy kid," Rebekah thought each time she read it. Then she would smooth out the creases in Aiden's face and return the clipping to the drawer.

Author's Note

Although this book is a work of fiction, bullying and harassment are real problems for gay, lesbian, bisexual, and transgender students in America's schools. For more information, including how students can help to create safe schools for everyone, visit the Gay, Lesbian and Straight Education Network at www.glsen.org.

Acknowledgments

With deepest gratitude, I acknowledge the team at Eerdmans Books for Young Readers, especially editor Shannon White, whose insightful questions propelled the book to a higher level and whose kindness during the pre-publication year will never be forgotten. And I remain indebted to those who read drafts of the manuscript and supported the book in countless other ways: Rachel Givner, Gwen Glazer, Kirsten Green, Brooke Kenny, Phyllis Mass, Elizabeth McBride, Meredith Narcum Tseu, Melissa Schiffman, Chad Tanaka, and Farrar Williams.

I am also grateful for the kindness shown to me during my AmeriCorps year in the Appalachian mountains, a year that inspired the setting (though not the characters or events) in this novel. There are too many people to list here, but I continue to think of you all.

Finally, I acknowledge the invaluable contributions of my family members: those who scratched their heads when I went off to the mountains and those for whom the mountains have always, in some way, defined me. I love you all.